Gone

G o n e

A N o v e l

M a r t i n   R o p e r

Henry Holt and Company

New York

Henry Holt and Company, LLC
Publishers since 1866
115 West 18th Street
New York, New York 10011

Henry Holt® is a registered trademark of Henry Holt and Company, LLC.

Library of Congress Cataloging-in-Publication Data
Roper, Martin.
Gone : a novel / Martin Roper—1st ed.
p.   cm.
ISBN 0-8050-6775-2 (hb)
1. Irish—New York (State)—New York—Fiction.   2. Dublin (Ireland)—Fiction.
3. New York (N.Y.)—Fiction.   4. Married people—Fiction.   5. Adultery—Fiction.
I. Title.
PR6118.O64 G66   2002
823'.92—dc21   2001039113

Henry Holt books are available for special promotions and
premiums. For details contact: Director, Special Markets.

First Edition 2002

Designed by Betty Lew

Printed in the United States of America

1   3   5   7   9   10   8   6   4   2

For Margaret

And what you thought you came for
Is only a shell, a husk of meaning
From which the purpose breaks only when it is fulfilled
If at all.

T. S. Eliot

Gone

Ruth

I put the telephone down and know Ruth is in the last moments of her life. There have been telephone calls before at odd hours but never at four in the morning. I dress quickly and run out onto an empty Tivoli Road. It is dark and raining so heavily I am soaked by the time I get to where the car should be parked. I can't find it on the road. City of stolen cars. God is testing me. This is what Ruth will say and I try not to get angry but it is too late—I am shaking with rage. I look in my pocket for money to call a taxi and as I'm counting the money in my hand I remember that it's a different car I have while mine is being repaired. It's blue this new one but I can't remember the make. I find it parked behind the yellow sports car belonging to the bitch who had once complained about the noise coming from the flat. I had

confronted her about it, telling her I had no radio let alone a
television. It's other sounds, she had said, like someone in pain. She
had the gall to look me in the eye but when I asked her what she
meant she just said it kept her little girl up nights. Tell her it's not
pain, it's pleasure, I had said. You know pleasure, you're a married
woman. I had regretted that. I had seen her in the summer in the
garden with her excuse of a husband, seen the silence and the
weak attempts to be a family with their desolate daughter. Every
time I pass the soft roof of her sports car I want to slash it.

Ruth hated sentimental movies and I laugh at the appropriate-
ness of the rain. I turn the key in the ignition, and the cassette
player comes on abruptly:

> *The smell of fresh cut grass is fillin' up my senses*
> *And the sun is shining down*
> *on the blossoms in the avenue*
> *There's a buzzin' flyin' around*
> *the bluebells and the daisies*
> *There's a lot more lovin' left in this world—*
> *Don't go! Don't leave me now, now, now*
> *While the sun is smilin'*

I turn the music off and wonder if I should have called
Ursula—she is visiting her father in Pontoon and won't be home
until later this evening.

The roads into the city are bare and still I drive carefully. I stop
at red lights and wait on the quiet, wet roads. The August dawn
is coming. She will not wait for the morning, she will leave now,
in the darkness. *Don't go yet.* She has been dying of cancer for
seven years, and many times I wished her dead so her misery

would end. And mine. I wish I had the courage to overdose her
on morphine rather than go on. The windscreen wipers are
exhausted with the rain. Don't crash. Just get there. I drive
deeper into the city. It is a Tuesday bank holiday and the first
trickle of workers are mournfully beginning the week. I am going
the wrong way. I have been so used to going to the hospital to
see her. Last Thursday morning the hospital had called me at
work and told me to come in immediately. I had been called
before like that and was reluctant to drop everything if it wasn't
urgent. A week ago, Canning, the hairynosed fucker I had for a
floor manager, had asked me how many miraculous recoveries I
expected my sister to make. Not many more, I had said. But the
nun spoke calmly and quietly on the telephone and said, yes, she
said, yes you should come now. She wants you to come now to
sign the papers. She wants to be moved from the hospital to the
hospice. She is nineteen.

    I slow down to get a sense of where I am going; my mind is
blank and I drive without knowing where I am going, hoping
something will click eventually. I am not meant to be with
Ursula. If it was meant to be she would be here now. It is an
absurd thought but instinct tells me it is true. I feel already we
have left each other, that all there is left is to say the words of
leaving. Harold's Cross. The hospice is in Harold's Cross. Either
through Ranelagh or Donnybrook, one of them. There is only
the sound of the windscreen wipers and the tyres cutting
through the wet roads. The silence in the car is heavy and I turn
the stereo on again:

> *you can't leave now—don't leave now . . .*
> *if you get there I know you'll like it . . .*

I switch it off. The traffic light is red and turns green but I do not move. I start crying. The light turns red again. Then I feel her spirit touch me, a faint, warm embrace falling on me and I feel her faint kiss softly on my cheek. I feel a surge of relief run through me and then it is gone: I know she is dead now.

Darkness has almost completely left the sky when I park the car in the *Ambulance Only* space outside the main doors. The doors, usually open, are closed to the morning chill. I step into a churchlike stillness. A nurse is walking down the corridor. I take to the stairs, falling up them three at a time. It is futile to hurry but the legs are oblivious to what the heart already knows. As I come off the last step onto the landing, a young nurse, barely twenty, is standing near the window. She raises her palms to slow me down, and then changes her mind and drops them as if they are annoying her. Her face is taut with the struggle to find words. She looks as if she had been left in charge and is not quite ready for the job.

—Are you for Ruth?

—Yes. It's okay. I know.

—I don't even know your name. Are you her husband?

—She doesn't have a husband. I'm her brother.

I walk past her towards the ward.

—She's not there.

For an instant I think perhaps she means she is in the corridor with a suitcase ready to go home. Then she moves her hand to her mouth and I know I am right in thinking her dead. It is disturbing that she has been moved already. It has begun, the whole grisly business of the body.

—God, she was so young, she says.

The nurse is crying and I go to her and hug her shaking body.
When I look at her, her face is blotchy. My eye catches her name
tag, the same name as my sister. The strange serendipity of life
seeping into us, swirling around us.

A mass of pillows sit her half up in the bed and she looks like
she has a dozen times when she has fallen asleep this way, only
she is completely still. I almost speak to her. Such stillness in
death. I want to joke with her about the nurse crying. There is a
sheet of paper in a clear plastic folder on the bed underneath her
hands. I lift the sheet and touch her fingers: they are cooling.
The Lord is my shepherd. Jaded words of comfort on the sheet,
put there not for the dying but for the living come to mourn their
dead. I put my hand on the side of her warm face and kiss her and
then I lie down on the bed beside her and hold her. We were in
Grannie's house the last time I held her, reading from the Flannery O'Connor collection. I hated reading those grim and meaningless stories to her but she relished them. She had fallen asleep
on my arm and I awoke then to her calling my name through
clenched teeth.

—What is it?

—Basin.

It is too late and the bile, as yellow and as slippery as egg yoke,
coughs out of her mouth onto the blanket. So strange, no gurgling intestines, nothing but the heaviness of death and a face
without pain. I am frightened for her that she was alone in those
last minutes. She had been awake, I am sure. Somehow I know
she didn't go in her sleep. She had been awake, waiting for it. I
shiver and still myself not wanting to pass my own fear into her.
Her face is flushed with the life having left her. At last all the pain

is gone from her. The heat of life leaving her now. I pull the blanket up on her to keep her warm and imagine her opening her eyes, calling me a gobshite.

I'm done, she had said, last Thursday, just before she asked me to sign the transfer papers. I don't want to die but this body is no use. I'm not giving up. You know that? I nod. I am staring out at the traffic on Eccles Street. A busy morning outside but here everything is quiet. The dirty windows can't be opened and the air is dead. I tell her she has done everything she could. This is the last road. We all take it.

—I'm not giving up. This stupid body is no use. Everything else is grand. You know I'm not giving up?

—You're not giving up. We're fellow travellers. I'm going back to America, out of here. I'll miss you. I'm scared of you dying.

She smiles a long smile and lifts up her hand for me to come closer.

—I'm glad you said that. You're the only one who ever cared.

—He cares too. He just doesn't know what to say.

I help her up then, to the bathroom. She holds on to my shoulder as she squats over the toilet bowl. Nothing. The morphine dulls the pain but constipates her. So she stops taking it and then the pain comes back. This is why I hate the medical profession. There must be something they can do with such a simple problem. Fuckers all of them. This is why I hate that we have no money, hate that my father drilled into us the mantra of the poor: money doesn't buy happiness. No, but it eases the pain.

She is cold now. I get up and sit on the bed. I want to leave the room quickly. I am afraid of sitting with her here, dead, afraid of a dead body that is Ruth. I put my hand on her cold leg and close my eyes and listen to the candle flickering and hissing on the windowsill. For a brief moment I remember sitting in a circle and staring at a candle when I was on retreat with the priesthood, when I was on the verge of my novitiate. Eight years ago. Before all this. It had been the calmest I had ever been. Her coldness is coming through the blanket. There are voices outside, my father is asking the nurse to speak up because of his hearing. His voice rings down the corridors of the hospice, waking the light sleepers who will know another one of them is gone. They are all waiting, all wondering who it is who is gone. My father starts to cry loudly. In he comes clutching the nurse as if he is facing an accident about to happen. His emotion flaps wildly and the peace scatters. A sister appears and offers him a seat in an adjoining room. She touches him on the shoulder, touches me on the shoulder, smiles a radiant smile and strokes my head as if I am a child. God bless you, she says. How often I have heard these words and they mean nothing. But this morning, coming from her, I feel their meaning, and feel there *is* a God, and God is here now, waiting and watching. I follow my father into the waiting room.

The nun brings tea and sandwiches. The room is bright now, the sun is up. The nun asks if I would like something else. My father looks up from the sandwich he is eating, his eyes guilty as if caught in the middle of indecency. He looks as if he would eat anything, as if he is under orders. The nun comes back with a bottle of Paddy and a glass. I drink the whiskey and it burns into my stomach. My father grins and hands me a sandwich. It is nearly eight when we leave. The morning traffic is heavy and I drive carefully, trying to avoid the heaviest of it. This isn't the shortest way, he says irritably. I tell him it's the best way with the morning traffic. We start to argue. I am thinking of the last week-end Ruth and I had together, alone at Grannie's house. I had picked her up on a Friday evening after I was finished work. She would spend the week in the hospital and then have a weekend out. She was desperate to get out of my father's house when she stayed with him. The television was always on and there was always endless talk. Him sitting there not watching the blaring screen. I was tired that Friday night, I was doing badly at work. Gerry was covering for me. Canning was in shit form because the Japs had returned a consignment. I had argued with Ursula. Despite her understanding and support, she was jealous of the time I spent with Ruth. For as long as we've been together all she has known is this illness. I suppose it could have just been that she was tired of not seeing me and when she did it was hardly worth the seeing. My depression showed most clearly with her. This was another weekend when I would disappear with Ruth and come back Sunday night, tired and loathing the idea of hav-ing to get up on Monday morning to face those morons. Ruth wanted a Chinese take-away. I asked her for directions and she said turn left and I did. No, left, she said. That *was* left, I said banging the steering wheel and she put her hand to her mouth for me to stop. She opened the car door and vomited onto the road. I am thinking about this as my father argues in the car over the shortest way home. He can't drive and has no understanding of roads. The longest way is sometimes the shortest, I say to him. We are both quiet, alone in the loss of her.

When I leave him at the house he is frantic with wanting to know where I am going. I tell him I want to be alone. I want to go to Grannie's house. I am desperate to be with Ruth, to be with what is left.

The sunflowers Ruth planted in the garden are in full bloom. I go around the back and let myself in through the kitchen. There is still the sharp odour of fresh paint. I had been painting the place while she was in the hospital as a surprise. She had done well that week and got out early, before I finished. When she came in the back door she had to run out because of the paint fumes. The chemotherapy made smells repugnant to her.

The paint job was never finished, the pink undercoat grimy with use. We had a phone installed in the house but it never rang, was never picked up. There was never any emergency. The drama of her dying was sirenless. I sit for a while in Grannie's chair looking at the telephone. I lean over and pick it up, expecting it to be dead; clear electric buzz. There is tremendous tranquillity inside the walls. Finally, I rouse myself to go. There is the funeral to do.

The first thing my father wants to do is to get rid of everything. We drive to Grannie's house and I begin loading all of Ruth's belongings into the boot of the car. We shove everything into black plastic bags. He wants to take it all to the nuns, wants to wipe her out. I keep removing things from the boot—her Bible, the Flannery O'Connor stories, the three packs of Dunhill she didn't get to smoke, her old pink jumper—and putting them on the backseat to save. Bits of her. Daddy is saying *fuck* quietly to himself. I laugh at the strangeness of hearing bad language coming out of his mouth and he glares at me. He is spending a long time walking around the house picking up things and putting them down again. He's looking for a system. Room by room we fill bag after bag and carry them out to the car. Fuck, fuck, fuck.

After we drop the full load at the convent we drive to Dolly-mount strand where I used to go with Ruth from time to time. We would park the car close to the water's edge, and sit there with the doors open, listening to the sea come in, and when the waves began to lap around the wheels of the car we would reverse back slowly, waiting again for it to catch us, reversing back a few feet at a time, toying with the risk of sinking into the softening sand. We would sit and listen to the waves. I tell him this now as we walk the length of the pier.

—What did you talk about?

—Nothing.

—Yous must have talked about something.

No. We didn't talk much at all. I asked her if she'd go to that clinic in America if we got the money. She said she wouldn't make it. He doesn't believe me, thinks I'm holding some lumi-nously private moments to myself, that I'm selfishly cherishing the profound and intimate conversations. But I am being honest. There was nothing left to say. We stop at the end of the pier and Daddy looks up at the statue of the Virgin Mary.

—Fuck all use *she* was when she was needed.

He looks at me, face of a naughty boy who has gone too far. As we walk back down the pier we link each other. It is the first time I have ever linked him and he is crying. I want to be far away from him. I have no stomach for his sadness. I will leave and not come back. He is ashamed of his tears. Tears have crum-pled him into nothing. People are walking along Clontarf prom-enade. Dogs barking and chasing each other. All the years I cycled out here with him to work in the houses of the middle class I hated. He must have hated them too, the money they held so tightly. You wouldn't do the window out the back if there's a drop of paint left? No problem Mrs. The silent years of childhood by his side hating them and smiling at them and taking ten pence into my hand and saying oh thank you very much Mrs. There was one other time he cried I remember. One Christmas Day many years ago. It was the second Christmas after our mother had left. Ruth and I had been fighting. Suddenly he started crying and the two of us stopped and looked up at him, frightened that if he gave in to it all we would be alone. How friendless it was for him after she left, a life without adults.

We go to Jennings Funeral Home at the Five Lamps in North Strand. We have passed this way hundreds of times on our way into town to buy paint in Wigoders of Mary Street. I won't always be around, you know that, he would say. You and your sister will have to take care of each other. That's why you shouldn't be fighting. There's no one else will give a shite about you when you're in trouble but your sister. Jimmy Mulligan works in Jennings and ask for him when I kick the bucket. I could not imagine him being dead—he was too big a man. As we grew older and he would tell us he wouldn't always be there, that he'd be going soon, we would ask him when he was going and did he want a packed lunch. Fierce funny you are.

Mulligan sits with his hand in his chin listening about Ruth's long illness. Already the story of her life coming out of my father's mouth is sounding worn-out at the elbows. Mulligan says yes, it's been very hard on you, Francis.

—She was only young. The wife and now her.

Ma isn't dead, I want to say. She's worse than dead. I wish the slut was dead. He has some infuriating need to explain all to strangers. He knows Mulligan thirty years but they are strangers to each other, and yet he doesn't understand this. Maybe he does, maybe he understands everything. I don't know my father at all. Mulligan can tell I'm judging him, he takes my expression in slowly, pretends not to notice. He lets my father talk until finally he is out of words, sitting there like a toy that's motor has stopped. Mulligan lifts up his book of coffins.

—We want the cheapest.

Mulligan nods at me and manages to ignore me at the same time. He puts the book in front of us. He begins to explain the various features of the coffins.

—The cheapest.

He smiles tightly and nods.

—This is a nice one, he says, tapping the book with a finger. Cheapest, too. It has gold-plated handles, but of course you won't be able to lift the coffin by them. They're plastic. Glued on. But it's a solid piece. Fine wood.

He rubs his nose with a knuckle as if he's a farmer selling a pig. He's not going to spend much longer with us. He can see Daddy is ready and he slithers towards the sale. The word obsequious was invented for undertakers. He starts to list what else we might need.

—Nothing else, Sir.

—You'll need a hearse?

—No.

—Ah Stephen the man's right. Unless we put her on a pram, he laughs to make Mulligan feel more comfortable. The family disease—the effort to make strangers comfortable, to be liked. We decide on a hearse and one limousine for the two of us. Aunt Muriel will travel in it too. The bill is just over twelve hundred pounds. Six hundred for the hearse alone. We stare at Mulligan and my father repeats the price of the hearse.

—We didn't have her insured.

—Yes. Well maybe someone has a car. A friend. That way you'd save on the limo.

—No. It's alright. We'll manage. We'll have the limo, right?

Daddy looks at me, pleading with his eyes to go along. I stare at Mulligan, wanting him to understand he is profiting from grief. Outside, we argue about the need for the car. I'm worn-out and agree with him, will agree with anything now.

The priest wants to meet with me to arrange the reading at the funeral and to say a few words. Father Macken had visited Ruth from time to time at the hospital, uninvited. She had no intention of giving her soul to him, and this is how it was, he would sit by her bed and pray for her, hoping she would come back to the church she had left. She had abandoned Catholicism, but not God. If she could have given Father Macken her soul, she would have, she would have emptied the brown paper bag of his grapes and slipped her soul into it for his care. The presbytery is ringed with barbed wire. He's been broken into five times the previous year. I ring the bell on the outside gate and wait. He comes down the steps slowly, even though he's a young man. He's walking with the gravitas of the bishop he wants to be. He shows me into the sitting room and goes through the selected readings for the funeral service. I dislike them all and tell him so, and that, more importantly, my dead sister would not have cared for them. He seems to be as offended by me referring to Ruth as dead as he is by the effrontery of considering any passage of the Bible inappropriate. He suggests I take a few minutes to find a suitable passage and leaves the room, wiping the palms of his hands on his thighs.

I look around the room for the first time: heavy floral wallpaper, bookshelves, dining room table with a vase of hydrangeas on it. I thumb through the Bible, uninterested. Nothing is suitable. I shut the Bible quickly and open it and stick a blind finger on the page—it is from the Book of Psalms, Lamedh. Your word, O Lord, is eternal. This would do, anything would as long as it wasn't chosen by prickface. I wait long minutes for him to return. Reluctantly, he agrees to the reading but is unhappy I want to say a few words as well. It might upset people, he says. Might upset me not to say them, I say. He suggests I say my few words afterwards at the cremation and not in the church but I explain I want to say something to the neighbours who will not be at the cremation. He will give me the nod, he says.

My father disappears down to the church the morning of the funeral. Muriel and I wait an hour for him to show up so we can all go in the car. The doorbell rings. Ursula. Muriel lets her in. No love lost there. My father will be talking to whomever will listen, anything to distract himself. After getting the bloody limo it sits there with no one to go in it. I invite Ursula to accompany us in the limousine but she says it wouldn't be appropriate for her to go as she isn't family. I tell her I would like her to come with us but she says it is not the right thing to do. I am sick of her rigidness, her knowing what's the right thing to do. We take the limousine to the church and she follows in her car. When I look around at her I can see the strain on her face. In a way, she is the only person outside the family who cares. She had brought rich soup to the hospital, lotion for Ruth's bedsore legs, simple things that no one else did. But none of that matters—I am burning with dislike for her. Appropriate. What am I doing with a woman who says *appropriate*? People are blessing themselves as our car passes. This is what the black limousine is, a mobile stage for us to act out our sadness.

He is outside the church talking to neighbours.

—This is Mrs. White and Mrs. Grey. Do you remember them? You were only knee high to a grasshopper. I smile at them. Yes I remember. The bitch who made us eat our lunch in the garage and the bitch who didn't pay us for over a month. The Whites, the Greys, the Browns, the Blacks, Protestants so dull they couldn't pick good colours for names let alone their houses. He tells them Ruth and I had been very close, and they nod gravely affording me what they hope is a suitable degree of reverence. Mrs. O'Neill, the wife of the press secretary for the Taoiseach, is there. Didn't pay us at all for the last job. That's how they have it, is all my father said. But we'll get our reward in the next life, he'd say.

—You're needed in the church.

He looks at me as if he is about to be executed. Outside the church the pallbearers are starting to take the coffin out of the hearse. I ask them to wait and call my uncles over. I remember playing with them as a child but haven't seen them since they moved to the Southside. The four of us lift the coffin. We buckle briefly under the weight of her. As we walk up the aisle I notice how full the large church is, fuller than it should have been. Who were these people, come to mourn a woman they did not know?

Father Macken is talking and no one is listening to him. His voice carries no understanding of Ruth. He mentions Joan of Arc and Jesus Christ and the joy of suffering and I glance at Muriel and smiles spread across the two of us. He comes down to shake hands with the family during the service, and he skips me. I am astonished I am passed over, and Macken becomes more human, smaller, less priestly.

The time for the reading comes and I walk soberly up to the altar, open the Bible at the section marked by the brown taper and stare at the words and start to read and then stop, only slowly absorbing that it is one of the passages Macken had chosen.

—This isn't it, I say, and then look up shocked that I have said it aloud into the microphone. People stare. I look down and pray to find the passage. I cannot remember where the section is. Lambeth. No, that's the place in Wales. I had picked it so quickly. Then I turn the page and there, like a small miracle, it is. I read it carefully, and when done, I turn and look at Macken. Macken looks at me blankly, without resentment, the look of foe respecting foe.

The service ends and he does not give me the nod to say the few words. Muriel puts a hand on me and says to let it go. But I am not going to let it go. I am not being bullheaded. I am cold inside and still. I am doing what Ruth would have wanted. The priest is stepping off the altar, people are starting to walk up the

aisle to pay their respects, the pallbearers are making their way
to the coffin. I ask them to wait and they look from me to
Macken and when they get no sign from him they move forward.
I tell them not to touch the coffin. Macken wets his lip with his
tongue. My hands tremble with the look in the man's eyes. What
was wrong that he would not allow us to grieve in our own way?
I ask him where I should stand and he goes up and pulls the
microphone down off the altar. I unfold the sheet of paper I have
made notes on. I begin to remember her. Her patience with the
scum we have for neighbours. Her courage, her humour, her
despair, her love of God but not of organised religion. That does
it. Macken grabs me by the shoulder and pulls me but I push him
gently and continue. Then it's over. I've had my say and feel foolish. I want to carry Ruth out as we carried her in but am over-
whelmed with the people gathered around us. People I don't
know, people I do know and don't like, people who don't like me,
people who didn't like Ruth, they line up with their words and
their reasons for being there. Uncle Aidan, a man uncomfortable
with touching, embraces me.

I spend as much time as possible alone, but it is difficult to put
Daddy out of my mind. I am full of resentment towards him—I
tried for a long time to show him that this day would come and he
needed to talk to Ruth before she died. Week after week we had
sat on either side of her bed talking to each other, and she watched
us as if watching a game of Ping-Pong. How well-intentioned but
impossibly stupid I was to foist my understanding on him. It was
like this with everyone who came to visit her. The tentative *How
are you?* was never really a question at all. Ruth said hospital is an
unbarred prison. You enter, they take away your clothes, force a

routine on you, force muck they call food down you, make you share your days and nights with strangers, and the visitors, the visitors are the worst of all; slinking in, fear mingled with guilt, and out with embarrassment, relief trailing behind them.

The scattering of the ashes. I telephone him to arrange it. That's taken care of, he says. It is not even a week since her death. Paddy Howard took me out to Howth and we did it there, he says. I am glad he has done it that way. I need to hate him. Now I can leave Ireland finally, without guilt. It's as if Ruth has died twice and I have been excluded from this more private funeral by my own flesh. I hate him. I hate him because I am closer to Ruth than anyone, no one could love her as much as I do. I didn't think she could be loved more, even by the man who had helped bring her into the world. The vision of Daddy climbing a hill with his favourite customer to scatter his daughter's ashes sundered the idea of who I was in the family. He had lost his only daughter. He, who had brought her into the world, and raised her, he alone would watch her leave.

Only in New York years later did I begin to feel how wrapped up in myself I was, and when I told Holfy about this, she told me I must ask him what happened. I couldn't. Daddy had been through enough. I did not want to bring him more pain. This is only partly true. Fear and anger kept me quiet. I was not certain what I was afraid of but I knew I was angry for being left out. Five years later when I did ask him, I did it in Lone Tree, four and a half thousand miles away. Daddy had only recently decided he could afford a telephone and when it rang he associated it with danger and expense. He went quiet when I asked him about the scattering. I don't remember about all that, he says. The contempt I am trying to rid myself of rises up. He isn't even sure where the hill is.

—Paddy didn't walk all the way with me if that's what you mean. I walked on a bit on my own. It was a lovely day. Very still. There wasn't a sound or a murmur anywhere. I got to where I thought was a good spot and said a little prayer, and I opened the urn and scattered the ashes. But just then a wind came up and blew the ashes in my face. It got in me eyes. Paddy said to go for a pint but I didn't think that was right so he drove me back to the house.

I am shaken when he tells me the story, not because of the wind, I can dismiss that as pure chance, but because he tells it so succinctly. I understand in the calmness of his voice how I have wronged him. He is an old dog after being abandoned by his owner and having no understanding of why he is alone. I see him differently through the few letters he has sent to me in America. Tentatively, humbly, he offers his son advice. He says he knows nothing of life and says he makes many mistakes. His age shows in the shakiness of his inelegant handwriting. His letters with their dates and their regular indentations at the beginning of every paragraph remind me that he is not just from a different generation; he is a man from a different era. And, despite the poverty he endured in the early years, he had held us together as a family. Nothing, not even our mother broke our family. Nothing, except death.

My mind died for a long time during her illness, and immediately after her death. I thought of her every day after she was cremated, thought of her as ashes. Every night my last thought was her in the coffin in the mortuary at the hospice. She had been alone there. I cannot shake from my mind that she was still alive then, and scared. Thought of her as dead flesh, as ashes, as gone.

The Sunday before she died I took her out to the front of the hospice and wheeled her down to the Grotto. She was running out of cigarettes, and I said I'd go around to the shops to get her some. I walk down the long drive, and, as soon as I turn the bend, run. She might die there and then in the wheelchair. She is weaker than I have ever seen her. The shopkeeper is chatting amiably to a customer who is wearing a pink hat. Why remember that pink hat when I can't remember the sound of her voice? While I wait for the shopkeeper to be done talking I pull some sweets off a shelf. Maybe she would like some chocolates. Biscuits, too. A Sunday newspaper. When the man finally serves me I ask for eighty Dunhill. Always Dunhill when she was in the money. I shove them in the bag and rush out. No matches. I run back and throw ten pence on the table and shout *matches* at the man who has returned to his conversation with the pink hat. I stop running at the bend in the drive, slow to a fast walk. Her head is down, her chin on her chest, asleep. A cigarette, trailing smoke, held loosely between her fingers. I say her name quietly and she opens her eyes slowly, like a cat waking from a hot sleep. The cigarette drops from her hand. She can tell from my face I am thinking how close the moment is. She looks ashamed of herself, of the indignity of dying, dying before she becomes a woman. She reaches down to pick up the burning cigarette off the tarmac and stops halfway, and as she does I can see her as a teenager crouched for the four-hundred-metre relay, digging her spikes into the hard grass for leverage, the fastest finisher in the school. She could be behind thirty metres by the time she was passed the baton and still hit the tape first. I pick up the cigarette and hand it to her, but she shakes her hand minutely.

—Sick of being sick, she says.

The night before she died I slept badly. Sadness finally exhausted me and I dozed. My mind fell in and out of sleep, in and out of dreams, morphine drugging Ruth into death, Ruth calling for our mother, Ruth calling, screaming an animal scream at death. I thought I should take her out of the hospice tomorrow and bring her to Tivoli Road. I thought about getting up now and visiting her. It was nearly three in the morning. I felt her mind awake, felt it moving through me, through the streets, through the houses, felt her breathing a goodbye, each breathing in a heavy triumph and each breathing out a resignation; soon it would be the last breathing out, no more words would be spoken, no more thoughts would form. She would be lucid. Everyone asleep in the hospice, the night nurse listening to the radio in the curtained office. I fell back asleep and in my sleeping, she slipped away. Nothing bit like that single regret.

Whenever I look at her photograph on my desk I freeze and am able to think of nothing, not even her. Eventually, I begin to notice the photograph less and less. The funeral begins to occupy my thoughts. I question my motives. Was I no different from the priest who wanted to save her soul in his fashion when I wanted to celebrate her memory in mine? Perhaps I was looking for attention by dramatically and poignantly making a stand at the funeral with the priest. Perhaps I was no better than the hypocrites who shook my hand in their effort to assuage their guilt. I wasted so many days not writing when I promised her I would write every day. The most horrific truth is forgetting, forgetting and going on. But there is no other choice. The only option is to live a fiercely joyous life knowing full well that misery leans against every street corner.

Ursula

It must be easy for fiction writers—to make it all up. To shape reality and make it conform to some vision of the way it should be. Truth is not easy. I thought it was, that facts made it so. How could Ursula, she who was so vital, be gone? After Ruth's death, I thought life would be easier, that death hardens one against pain. The endless well of naïveté. There is no chronology. I cannot weave them together.

We go for a walk up the hill of Howth. Ursula is coquettish, looking for my hand on the steep rises. It's not like her and I like her more for it. We sit on a boulder and look out to sea. Gulls are squawking over a mass of brown in the blue sea.

—Enough to put you off your lunch.

All I can think of is kissing you. You turn and stare at me, a serious face.

—Kiss me.

I kiss her and her lips are lovely. She kisses back. We kiss and kiss and I burp in the middle of it I'm so nervous.

—Pig.

—It was an accident.

She pushes me on my back. We kiss and find each other. Her buttocks tight against her jeans. I run my hand down her leg. Her leg is hard as rock. Sweet, sweet touches. She raises herself off me and smiles intriguingly. She sits back and pulls her trouser leg up to the knee and knocks on the leg. She nods at my astonishment.

—Where does it start?

She karate chops above the knee.

—And the other one?

—That too. No, the other one is fine.

She shows a white ankle for proof.

—I never guessed.

She shrugs.

—No one knows. Except my family.

—What happened?

—Cancer. Let's eat. It's no big deal. At least not to me.

I open the basket we have brought and I think about telling her about Ruth, about the cancer, but decide against it.

—Me neither. Leg? Of chicken.

—Weak.

I knew then I would ask her to marry me.

⊸∾ ⊸∾ ⊸∾

At work I find the slow constant hiss of the gun comforting. Ursula is getting ready for her job, back at the flat. Wife: how wonderful to have a wife. I imagine her dressing, smile at the pleasure of knowing her routine. I marvel at the work. The paint fanning over the black plastic frame turning it metallic silver. I swivel the jig to paint the next side, arcing the gun to cover the curved edge of the television frame. Love this job. It takes a special kind of concentration to paint television escutcheons five hundred times a day. Set the record last month with 578 in a single shift. Over six hundred if they included defects. Thinking of the defects, my skill wanes. The siren goes and Gerry and I drop the guns with relief.

The other workers scuttle across the factory floor to be first to the vending machines. We make our way to the toilets. We peel off the cotton gloves, the hoods, the face masks, and wash. The paint spray finds its way through to the skin, regardless. I blow my nose and decide not to think about the paint—it's approved by the minister for health himself. Gerry spits into the urinal.

—Want anything?

I shake my head.

—What are you smiling at?

—Nothing.

—Go on.

—Ursula is my wife.

—You're smiling at that? Sap. If that fucker Canning doesn't lay off me I'll knife him.

—Relax. You'll be a manager too one day and then you can be a bollocks.

I sit in the cubicle and stare at the chipboard door. The same coarse talk out of them every day. *Did he drop the hand? I'd fucking kill him if he said that to me. Shut up you. Prick.* Got to get out of this poxy place. I'm about to swear when I stop myself. She warned me about my language. She has a habit of entering my thoughts when I'm on the edge of anger. The morning after the honeymoon. Lying in bed in the hotel. We were shocked with the drabness of the room. The place had seemed so grand, looking out onto the bay. I pretended its loveliness.

—It's old-fashioned without the niceness of old-fashioned.

I delight in her directness; a mixture of bluntness and shyness. It was a still, hot night and we slept with the blankets off us. Her naked body lying on its side, facing me. Raising my fingers to the mouth, afraid to touch her. Her breasts are heavy and happy; full of smiles. So many pleasures with her. I stare at her in the darkness. Are you dreaming of us? Of when we met?

I had just entered sixth year, and swear I will avoid girls until after the exams, not that I've even touched one, acne and shyness deterring me. We meet at the school dance. She is sitting there in a long black dress, watching everything. And I am watching her. A month later she lets me slip a hand under her blouse, and I hope she can't sense the trembling in my fingers. The gentleness of her breast; the nipple, hard as a nut. The consternation inside of me, knowing she is excited. The first time I touch her is in the park. We meet there after school and go to the back of the football pitches near the Basin. How she excites me. Her moaning frightens me but I can't bring myself to stop until her hand tightens about my wrist. A butterfly taking flight. My fingers on her stomach slipping beneath flesh and jeans, down into the wetness between her legs, thrilled by the pulsing of her cunt's heartbeat. Ripples there, minutes later.

I go to bed without having any tea or without studying. Under the blankets, breathing her in on my fingertips: Ursula. Her smell. Happier than the smell of grass after rain. This couldn't be the fishy smell other boys joked about. How little they knew. How little everybody knew. How was it that people could go about their lives after discovering such a smell?

Because I am studying for the exams, it is three torturous days before I see her again. As soon as we are alone in the park I bring my fingers to her lips.

—Smell.

She shoves my hand away and stares at the fingertips suspiciously.

—I'm not messing. Smell.

She lifts my fingertips to the wings of her nostrils and inhales.

—You've been smoking.

—It's not cigarettes. It's you. It's you. Your smell from Monday evening. When we were here.

She grabs my hand and lifts her nose a little as if sniffing herself from the air about us. She bends and kisses my fingernails; the undersides of my fingers; licks my palm. She kisses and licks the palm and bites it and I whisper it's nice and it's lovely and she better stop and she better stop now before it's nicer and she says yes, she will stop kissing this palm all the time and I plead and she says she will stop in one kiss's time and I say no you are to stop now and to marry me please.

Her stomach sags a little and it looks as if it, too, is fast asleep. I have an urge to kiss her navel but restrain myself, fearing I will wake her. I blush at the shock, only a few hours old, when she

had taken her bright red knickers off: she is sitting at the far side
of the bed with her back to me. She stands, straightening herself
the way she does on her good leg, and my eyes rest on the dark
triangle of hair.

—What is it?

I shake my head.

—What is it?

I count the stars on the carpet.

—Please don't go quiet on me. Not on our honeymoon. Please
don't say nothing to me.

—I don't know what to do.

My face is burning.

—I do.

I look up.

—I mean I've a fair idea.

She laughs and I laugh. She walks like a clown on stilts when
she hurries.

We move into the flat in Lower Dorset Street over Youkstetter
the pork butcher, after the wedding at the end of July. My father
had offered us a room in the house until we got some money
together but neither of us wanted to live at home any longer—
she had reached the end of her tether with her mother who had
just started to get into the swing of things with her fond-of-a-
drop lover, Mulvany, who was living there now. No job, going
around half naked, letting Ursula know with his eyes he'd do her
too. Lover: it was the first time I'd ever heard someone use that
word out loud, and it was silly coming out of her mother's

middle-class, middle-aged mouth. Lover: a word that should imply passion but in her implied only pretension and desperation.

Cats used to gather in the back yard and force the lids off the rubbish bins. We slept with the window closed so the stench wouldn't waft in on top of us. That first blistering August we left all the doors open so that air could crawl into the bedroom from the front room. Staring up at the ceiling half the night, cursing the trucks passing on their way up the North, and stopping me from sleeping.

All that was after the honeymoon; adoring the sight of her; her arched foot; ankle with the tiny tattoo of the green and red hummingbird; her bent knee; thigh widening out, heavy hips falling down to the waist. I reach across and kiss the bottom. I take a breath and softly kiss her breast and my heart sings that I can please her and she not even awake. I go to the bathroom to relieve myself. The noise of the sea coming in the open window taunts me, whispering truths between each wave. My face is tired in the mirror. I have the responsible cut of a husband about me. Maybe this morning I'll be able to keep it in her longer. The coldness of the tiled floor seeps into my feet. A new resolve floods me and I run hot water over my hands to heat them lest they're cold on her. I creep back and slip beneath the covers beside her warm body and kiss her face. She stirs. I push my tongue between her dry lips and hear them part like glued paper. She stirs. I lick the surface of her teeth; the smoothness of hard ice cream. Her eyes open and she smiles at me.

—Morning, husband.

I raise myself on an elbow, away from the sudden surprise of her sour breath. My mouth must be the same, reeking of the night. She reaches out her arms, a tired child wanting to be lifted. Yet when I enclose her, I feel as if I'm the child and I hide my face against the nape of her neck, hiding the embarrassment that comes with the pleasure of her. The scent of her lilac perfume. Her body next to mine is the heavens unfastening. Let me manage it properly this morning. My father having to do the janitor job in the school when things got difficult at home: having to work for the Thorntons as well and put up with being checked on all the time as if he was a child when he couldn't get painting work. How I love him so unquestioningly. I love her more though, love her more than I love my own father, and the treachery of it catches in my throat. The siren screams and I rouse myself from the reverie of the cubicle. I had started to pleasure myself but there is no time. Foul graffiti daubed on the back of the door. I stand and wince—my leg is gone asleep. She gets sore sometimes in the amputated leg. I rub my leg back to life. Back in the spray-painting booth I attack the work vigorously, taking care not to let the hose of the gun hit the painted frames. I will the day to end, to be home with her.

Bath Avenue

The house was on a corner, and although my father always said never to buy a corner house, we did. Everything that could be wrong with a house was wrong with this one: the roof leaked badly, the guttering needed replacing, there were broken windows and the frames were warped and rotten, the bath was cracked, the toilet solidly blocked, the wiring was lead and dangerous, the wallpaper was soaked with rising damp, the plaster would have to be hacked off the downstairs walls up to a height of four feet, the walls drilled and injected with chemicals, the brick then left bare for six months to dry out, and finally, the walls could be replastered. Floor and ceiling joists were rotten. A ceiling collapsed during the renovations, barely missing the gas

man and the builder. There was no heating. The gas cooker
failed the Bord Gáis test and it and the pipes to the street would
have to be replaced. We knocked down several walls to make a
large kitchen. It was a dark, musty house on a corner between a
middle-class and working-class area and everyone said not to
buy. We did what every estate agent hopes a couple will do: we
fell in love with what the house could be. The roof, even if it did
leak, was a mansard of sorts and gave the room that would be the
bedroom a romantic air heightened by a small window tucked
under the eaves and sloping slate. The house, like us, was full of
potential and hope.

 We were in love with notions of each other. We were in love
with opposites. She was a non-practicing Protestant with a
Catholic name and I was a non-practicing Catholic with a Protestant name. She was from a middle-class background that had
slipped a little after her parents divorced. I was from a lower-
working-class background but was now living in a middle-class
world. Neither of us ever wanted to have children. We were disil-
lusioned with Ireland. She was writing good poems and an insipid
novel. I was jealous of her expanding life and ignored the compet-
itive drive in her. She thought me funny and I never dared admit
how seldom she got the joke; besides, I was drawn to her serious
nature. So we bought the house made of the crumbling Dublin
yellow brick on Bath Avenue in Irishtown. We took photographs
of each other leaning against the *Sold* sign. She bought us matching key rings, two silver fishes. I made a joke about the religious
significance and she said that was not the point at all; we were two
faithful fishes swimming forever in a sea of sharks. This fish was
working the nightshift in the factory for the extra money. Sometimes Gerry would hit the emergency button and all the machines

would die and we would stand there listening to the silence in the factory and he would roll up the sleeves and the trouser ends of his overalls and he would hobble up and down in front of the booths reciting "The Love Song of J. Alfred Prufrock":

> *I grow old . . . I grow old . . .*
> *I shall wear the bottoms of my trousers rolled.*

We hired skip after skip, and filled them with the old belongings left behind after Anna Condron had died there. Post still came for the woman, now nearly three years dead. The world takes its time letting the dead go to their graves. Work led to work. There were problems we hadn't bargained for—even exceeding our happy pessimism about the state of the house. The water cistern in the attic burst, but only after the plumber had installed new pipes leading to it. These, time revealed, were insignificant problems compared to what was to come.

There were nice surprises. When we stripped the old plywood on the stairwell we discovered there were original posts hiding there. As the months passed and spring came and went, we learned what a beautiful garden Anna Condron had planted. Pale pink roses. Black-eyed Susans. Snapdragons. Flowers we could not name. Ursula found five hundred pounds under the carpet in old twenty-pound notes. I wanted to blow it. She saved it for our future. Our future.

So engrossed were we in the house that we ignored the children who gathered at the corner every day. Some of the mischief they got up to is the kind of mischief any group of bored children get up to: ringing the doorbell and running away, screaming at us as we came and went. But there was something else in the

air, a hint of menace. The children played football late into the
night under the street lamps. The ball banged repeatedly off the
gable. Even though we were exhausted we could not sleep with
the noise. Summer came and with it the school holidays and the
trouble escalated. I can't remember the first time I told the children to move away from the house and not make so much noise.
I can't remember when their language got worse and they went
from calling us silly names to more vulgar ones. I can't even
remember the first broken window. The children began to take
on individual identities. There was Larry. He was about six and
he was the youngest. He was put up to much of the trouble. I
watched Larry from the window as he tore the windscreen
wipers off the car.

There were many days when I talked with them as I loaded the
skip. They asked questions nonstop. They asked if we were married and for some reason I lied and said no. This marked us in
their eyes. Larry looked at me and said, Holy God will come
down and fuckin' kill ya if you're not married. Darina, one of the
tallest, about fourteen, would be pregnant soon. It was in her
eyes. Alan, a boy who held Ursula in great disdain. He spat at her
and called her a cunt. When he hissed the word cunt he meant it.
They made fun of the way Ursula spoke. They thought she was
American with her accent that was a mixture of her English
father and celtophilic mother. There was Sabrina and Joseph and
Elaine.

Something was happening every day now. A ball would be
banged repeatedly against the gable. A bag of rubbish thrown
over the back wall in on top of the new flower beds. Graffiti
sprayed on the side of the house: *Psychohead! Cuntface! Geebag!*

Ursula began to spend more and more time at the office. Her career with the *Tribune* was up and running. We had been married three years before we decided to buy the house. Almost as soon as we did I knew it was a mistake. It was her money that bought the house and although I tried to make up for it by working hard on the renovation I couldn't put it out of my mind that it was her house. During an argument about where we should put the cooker she snapped that it was her cooker and her house, not mine. I looked at her dumbfounded and her eyes dared me to question her. She had said it and even though I could see the regret in her face, I could see, too, the defiance of her mother, of being raised not to take shit from any man. It was over then but I didn't know it. No I knew it but I didn't want *over*. And without even thinking about it very much, I did what so many do, I began to look around for Ms. Next.

She never apologised about the cooker. It wasn't her style to apologise, too much of the father in her for that. Shoulders back, look them straight in the eye. Never complain. Never explain. Never apologise. By the time she calmed down she knew there was a coldness in me that was permanent. The inequality had been spoken. I didn't have the courage to confront her about it, and when later she offered to put the house in both our names I dismissed the idea. It *was* her house. And it was all exacerbated by the odd coincidence that her mother had a man living with her, a man over twenty years younger who was living off her. Mulvany had no job and did nothing around the house except leave dirty ashtrays and teacups strewn about the place. He was a drunk. There were no parallels drawn between mother and daughter. There weren't any—except the crucial fact that both

women owned their property and the men in their lives were
moneyless. It all lay there between us like a stillbirth. I began to
hate Mulvany unreasonably. I began to hate her father and her
mother for divorcing when she was four years old, hated her suspicion of men. Fear creating the thing it fears. I had to prove I
was not a bastard rather than just be who I was—someone who
loved her. I started loving her less. Only three years married and
the intimacy between us worn more than the wedding shoes that
I only wore on Sundays. We slept in the same bed but we never
touched each other. In the night, if I awoke and felt our buttocks
meet I moved away as if a hot poker was between us. I promised
myself I would never touch her again but desire got the better of
the both of us. Afterwards, I would lie there disgusted with
myself for being inside her.

One night there was a knock on the door. I got out of the bath
and towelled quickly to answer it. We were expecting her
mother. One of the neighbours was standing there, heavy mous-
tached, topless and wearing only a pair of jeans; a stupid, good-
looking, chest-tattooed piece of shit from head to toe. He was
smoking and he pointed his cigarette at me and said that if either
that bitch or me ever as much as looked at his children again he
would fucking kill us. I asked him to come in, hoping if he stepped
into the hallway he might calm down, but he stayed where he was
with one foot on the door saddle. He went on and on, called us
perverts, a word Sabrina used. He put a foot into the hallway.
The ash lengthened on his cigarette and his reluctance to tap it
on the carpet gave some hope he wasn't a complete maniac.

—Your children are ruining our lives.

I looked around at Ursula, astonished she was interrupting him.

—Shut the fuck up you.

—You shut up and learn to control your children.

—I'm warning you, I'll rip you from your cunt to your chin.

—Go ahead.

She stared up into his face.

—Go ahead if you're so brave. Rip me.

—I'm warning you if you as much as look at my kids.

—Rip me. Go ahead.

He walked away. She followed him down the garden path. He stopped and looked at her and she spat in front of him.

—The state of you with your shirt off. Best part of you ran down your mother's leg.

He stopped and turned and sneered at her, turned the corner and walked down Bath Avenue, passed our gable and out of sight. She never took her eyes off him.

—Jesus, what did you say that for? He could have killed us.

—You talk that way about them.

—About them, not to them.

We went to the Gardaí that night and reported him. There was nothing they could do except warn him. They could come when we called if the children were giving trouble but they couldn't arrest them, they were too young. There was nothing they could do. They advised us to get out. The world was a small place that night, our lives dictated by children.

The next day the bathroom window was broken. We replaced it. When I had finished repainting the frame it was broken again. I replaced it again. When other things happened I stopped

telling Ursula. My silence was not stoicism—I was ashamed I had
no control, that with each passing day I was less and less of a man.

It happened on a quiet Sunday morning. We were lying in bed,
still asleep. A ball thudded off the gable. Then it hit the window
by the bed. We had designed a stained-glass window that threw
pink and green light into the room. A sheet of unbreakable glass
was in front of it. The ball was thrown harder and harder against
the window. We lay there not talking, listening. Ursula was wiping her hand over her knuckles, slapping the back of her hand,
drubbing herself until I couldn't bear it and I jumped out of the
bed, pulled on my clothes and ran out. They were already out of
sight. I ran and ran and kept running, the heels of my shoes cutting into my sockless ankles. I ran through Irishtown and on into
Ringsend and there they were outside a shop, eating sweets.
They all saw me except Alan who had his back to me. I lunged at
the child and threw him to the ground. He screamed, defiance in
his eyes. I sat on him and held him by the ears. I wanted to lift his
head and bang it off the footpath. I wanted to bang it until he
stopped moving but I couldn't do it. If I could have murdered,
that was the moment when I would have done it. I hated myself.
I hated that the child under me was a child and didn't really
understand how he was tormenting us. He would grow out of it.
He would grow up and breed more of his own into the world. He
wouldn't remember the misery he caused us. I walked back to the
house. I sat down on the front step and started sweating and
shaking. I took a pack of cigarettes out of my trouser pocket. The
packet was crushed but none of them were broken. Little bastards. Little bastards. I lit the cigarette. People passed on their

way to Mass at the Church of the Star. I flicked the cigarette out
into the road. I'd enough of it. She was in the kitchen feeding the
cats when I came in.

—We're selling.

—No way. I'm not letting them win.

You can go if you like, she said. I nodded and I could see I had
nothing left then. She didn't hide her disgust, I was a coward in
her eyes. I *was* a coward. But I understood something she did not
about these people. I grew up with their like—she would not
win. There was no winning with them.

There were older boys on the corner later that day. Teenagers.
They were lining up and throwing stones at the back windows.
They were casual about it. They were in no hurry. She tele-
phoned the Gards and they said they would have a car around in
minutes. A window broke. Then another. I went downstairs and
walked out. I walked slowly towards them. There were about fifteen in all. The local children and these older boys who must
have been from Ringsend. They started to laugh. I didn't care
anymore. I stared at them one by one. They waited on me to do
something. I suddenly remembered the final scene from *High
Noon* and smiled. They burst out laughing as if reading my mind.
I did nothing but stare. As I stood there in the middle of their cul-
de-sac I realised that most of their houses looked out onto this
road. Their parents would be home from Mass now. They would
have had their Sunday dinner and be watching the television. I
could feel eyes, other eyes, on me. Some of them must be watching this. I had no idea what to do and as I stood there I knew that
with each passing second my impotence was growing in direct
relation to their delight. I turned and walked away. The stones
started to fly. I walked slowly with every fourth or fifth stone hitting

me. There were apples, too. They must have raided an orchard.
The apples bouncing and smashing off the road made it more
humiliating. I knew Ursula was watching from the window and
that, like me, she was at a loss. A stone hit me in the head and
then they stopped firing briefly, testing the moment. I kept walking, swallowing spittle in my throat. A squad car turned onto the
road and pulled up beside me. The boys scattered like startled
birds. The Gardaí chased and caught two of them. They were
taken to their houses. Both fathers said their sons had been with
them all afternoon and closed their doors. A cop told me I should
go up to the hospital to have my head looked at and it's only then
I feel an iciness at the back of my head. I wipe the back of my
hair and it's wet. Come on, says the cop, we'll drop you off. I tell
Ursula to stay put and finish the article she's working on.

I lie in bed stunned by the fear that has overcome me. Ursula
offers me a drink but I want nothing except silence. The stitches
are tightening in my scalp. I stare up at the sloping ceiling overhead and close my eyes. I am nine years of age and walking home
from dull, stupid school. I will be nine years of age forever. I'm
walking on the side of the road that the houses are on, glimpsing
at each window in case I can see something shocking—a man
doing the fox trot with an Irish wolfhound, an old woman shooting heroin, a baby painting itself purple, a couple smiling at each
other. Anything but dead curtains. I light a cigarette off the tip of
the one I'm about to throw away. I'm getting the hang of inhal-
ing. The railway, high on the embankment, runs along the other
side of the road. A rock bounces off the ground in front of me. I
keep walking. Another rock whacks off the footpath. I put my

schoolbag in my right hand as a shield. The rocks come faster
now. I look up. There are two boys walking along the tracks.
They are skimming the rocks down off the railway and onto the
road as if there is an ocean there. They seem bored, as if they
don't care whether they hit me or not. I keep walking. The road
is a mile long and whether I turn around and go back towards
school or go on for home makes no difference—I've about the
same distance to go either way. We're doing *Macbeth* in school. *So
steeped in blood.* I walk slower. Never let anyone see your fear, my
father has always told me. The inner city in the seventies is a no-
go area and showing courage is not so much a mark of foolish
heroism as it is a way of survival. It's normal. A rock hits me on
the hip. I keep my pace. I can sense their excitement. They're
wondering how far to go, each rock flying out further into an
infinity of malevolence. Something hits me on the side of the
head and I fight the urge to lift my hand to the soreness. I keep
walking as if I feel nothing. They are running now, running down
the tracks away from the edge of hate.

I don't know why they picked me. Perhaps because I walked
home alone. Perhaps because I didn't make friends. I liked poetry
and I wasn't going to run into school with a Dylan Thomas poem
as if I had discovered a two-headed frog. Nonetheless, I wasn't
prepared to sacrifice my integrity to be in the club. My integrity.
Nothing was as pure and absolute as the stubborn integrity of my
childhood self. But later I would get over that. To join the club,
not a named organisation but a constantly shifting but predictable world children invent. One had to go with the craze of
the moment—go on the mitch, set cats on fire, break windows,

force younger children to drink a jam jar full of piss. All of this interested me in theory. I liked to think about the boy drinking the urine, what was going on in his head. And what was going on in the head of the boy who forced it down the throat. But I despised them for their vindictiveness and never would be a part of it. Be your own man, my father always said. I wasn't sure what being my own man entailed. I thought it meant I *had* to be alone. My father took good care of us and I never doubted his word. So I joined no clubs. I stayed out of the gangs and that made me different. Inside, I wanted to be what every child wants to be: the same.

My father didn't believe in fighting. He told me a man's job was to show that men could be men without behaving like wild animals. One day in school Mooney picked on O'Reilly. O'Reilly was always picked on because he couldn't stop sucking his thumb. McNally, the science teacher, came into the classroom and broke the scrap up. But we all knew what it meant. Four o'clock outside the back gates. About sixty of us stayed back to watch. Mooney started right in to it. He shoved O'Reilly on the ground and kicked him in the head. He kept kicking him in the head and O'Reilly made no sound. We watched. Usually there was pushing and shoving and name calling and a bit of a punchup and everyone cheered until someone stopped it. This was different. Blood was coming out of O'Reilly's mouth and out of his ear. I couldn't bear it and jumped in. I woke up in Temple Street hospital. Mooney had pulled out an iron bar from his jacket and hit me with it once on the side of the head. I lost the hearing in my left ear. I never got in a fight after that.

◊· ◊· ◊·

Medbh calls to visit. I am out in the back chopping wood. It is a quiet day and I am loving the freshness of the air, the joy of being alone, the silence, the happiness of doing a bit of physical work. Each split of wood the skull of Darina, Alan, all of them.

—That's very macho for you, she says.

—How's it goin'?

—You're sweet. Ursula is lucky to have such a sweetie.

I invite her into the house and we sit by the fire and talk. I don't know her well and don't particularly like her. She is too certain of life. After a cup of tea and a bit of chat about the delights of having a home, she tells me why she is here. She is lonely. She misses being a single woman. We look at each other, both of us thinking the same thing, thinking about Brefini, her husband. She knows by my eyes that it's the wrong thing to say to me. I am sad for her, and feel I am getting old, learning to know that sharing such intimacy is not intimacy, it's nothing but a slide into collusion. I am learning slowly. She asks for my advice about a man her sister is interested in and I tell her I don't know. I don't know how to get a Rawl plug in a hole without bending it, how would I know about this man her sister wants. She thanks me for my advice, warms herself a moment longer by the fireside, rubbing her hands on her thighs, lingering to dispel the awkwardness between us, and then she leaves. She has no idea that she has offended me. It is nothing to do with Brefini, it is my own frail ego. Why should she think that a lighthearted comment about macho—or the lack of it—would be hurtful? Why would she think that calling me skinny or boyish or sweet could ever be construed as offensive?

For a woman to say she is envious of a man's skinniness is like complimenting an obese woman for her jolly nature. I get the message—it translates from compliment to insult in a finger click. To be called boyish translates as hormonally undeveloped. To be *sweet* is the trickiest one of all to handle because it seems innocuous. Here's the rub: women tell me men are not sweet. Women tell me men are bastards. So, somehow, even though sweetness *is* a virtue, one is less of a man for possessing it. My head begins to ache as if cold air is being forced through the healing wound. It was stupid to start working so soon.

This time Ursula agrees we should sell. I am worried for our safety. I want to protect her and know I can't. Besides, the truth is she is not the one in danger. If someone is going to be hurt it is going to be me. There is enough decency in this scum not to hurt a woman. We agree to work extra hard on the house to get it finished and put it on the market quickly. My attitude changes overnight. We had taken care to do everything as expertly as possible, staining the skirting boards four times, varnishing them four times. Now I take short cuts. She doesn't. She is still attached to the house; it has become her love. I grit my teeth when I hear her still sanding the downstairs skirting boards, the obsession with smoothness of door frames and windows and walls. I tell her again and again to hurry and not worry about the fine details. We have finished everything except the papering and painting. The paint tins sit in the kitchen waiting to release their colours. I open them and stir them into life. Yellow, pink, blue, green. Happy colours. I size the walls in the living room and watch the paste dry in. I plumb the wall over the fireplace.

—What are you doing?

She is standing in the doorway, wiping dust off her face.

—Lining the walls.

—They're not ready.

Her anger takes precedence over expertise.

—If you think they're not ready you can do it—you can do all of it. Wouldn't that be fun?

—Fine.

—It's not fine. You want to help? Stop being a know-all expert and just get it done. Now fuck off.

—Fuck off you.

—I should never have married a woman who couldn't say *fuck off* properly.

—And I should never have married a man who couldn't fuck properly.

—Maybe if there was someone worth fucking.

—She left your father a long time ago.

I climb the ladder, hold the roll of paper to the ceiling, let it drop until the roll hits the space between my toe and the wall, feel the precision of my father working in me. I measure the first length, lay it on the table and run the other lengths of paper off it. I am happy in my anger. Success lies in letting her go one better in insults and leaving silence the job of cutting her down. I paste the paper and let it soak in, then paste it again. She is still standing there, waiting for a reply. I start to whistle, the happy whistle of my father when he had to deal with customers looking over his shoulder. In his heyday he would have a room this size done in three hours. The door slams, and the house, empty of furniture, echoes with her hostility. I am halfway around the room when I notice I'm going the wrong way—the joins in the paper will show. No matter, they won't rise for months. We are decorating the house for someone else now. We are fighting more and more, the arguments only a break from the bitter silence. Despite her independence and staunch feminism she feels let down by the man in her life. I am a coward. I am running away. These are the things we don't talk about, the unsaid words that widen the gap in the bed.

She wants to ensure all the floorboards are secure before we put the last of the skirting boards down. I keep going with the lining paper, running it down to the floor. We work in inverse proportion to each other, the more corners I cut, the more care she takes in the details. I watch her comb her hair at night, as I have done every night for years. The slow rhythmical brushing, the decisive centre parting that I loved to watch irritates me. We would come to blows if it wasn't for exhaustion. She is still fighting the children in her head. The house is papered now, dressed from head to toe. One evening I come in and she has written poems on the walls in pencil. Sexton, Plath, Ozick, Rich, Bishop, Glück, Levertov. Poems pencilled neatly all over the house. The pencil will burn through the paint and I sit down under the weight of resentment. But she hasn't done it on purpose I suppose. Three coats will cover them, and then slowly, over the winter months, when the new occupants turn on the heating the poems will bleed through and reveal their past. I want to write poems too but can think of none. I caught this morning's morning minion. Dappled dawn. I go up to bed. She is already asleep.

I wake to the smell of paint. She is rolling the walls in the room that was to be her study. Bright yellow. Rolling wet sunshine. She should have done the ceiling first but I say nothing. All advice is accusation now. I go down and start the kitchen ceiling. Contentment settles in our working. I shout up if she wants tea and her yes sounds like the first casual word she has spoken in months. I go out and get fish and chips and we sit on the stairs eating them out of their bags. We talk about how much longer it will take. The papered walls insulate our voices; speech heavier now. I think about telling her how ashamed I am of my fear but don't. Work is the only refuge left in our marriage.

We go to Brefini's and Medbh's house on a Sunday afternoon to talk about books, a dull Dublin version of the Bloomsbury set. About a half dozen of her friends (only later would time teach me the sundering of friends) talk and talk, and the only aspect that appeals to me is the decadence of drinking wine in the middle of the afternoon. I hate the way they tear books apart for the sake of it. Everything for effect. They are like young barristers cutting their teeth. Today they are discussing Cormac McCarthy's latest book. Ursula and I had read it in bed together the night before. Rather, she read it and I occasionally read over her shoulder. We both hated it. Man's struggle with the Universe against an imponderable sunset. She finished the book late into the night. I remember listening to some of the locals coming home drunk. The next day battle ensues over the book. The men are attacking Ursula. I have learned to be careful and not to defend her for two reasons: I do not want it to seem I am defending her because we are a couple who have lost our intellectual identity for the sake of coupledummydom; and she has told me she is more than capable of taking care of herself. Lately, though, she has mentioned that I am too distant and so I decide to defend her. It is turning into the great tedious gender debate—the men liking the book and the women not—and I hope my erudite opinion will turn the argument around.

—Horseshit and sunsets in an America that doesn't exist.

—You haven't even read the book.

Everyone looks at her and then me. I smile my finest roguish smile. It doesn't hide a thing. I go silent and the men all laugh. On the way home I think about other times she has disappointed me, all of them as petty as this one. She asks me why I am silent and I can say nothing with the anger in me. She sighs, resigned to silence.

—You know what Medbh told me men want, Ursula?

—Tell me Stephen, what did Medbh tell you men want?

—Three things: To be fed from time to time, a good blow job, and never to be made look silly in public or talked about behind their backs.

—That's four.

—I didn't give a fuck about the book. I was supporting you.

—You lied. Arguments should be based on facts.

—That's the mistake women make in arguments with men. You think we work on logic. You can't beat men with logic. Men make the illogical sound logical. Get over it. But hey, if you want facts, we'll live on facts. *We will live with facts. Never expect me to defend you again. Never, never expect my trust.* The trailing unspoken ends of sentences. The ones that count.

It wasn't out of spite, the first affair with the Italian. It was more mundane and more pathetic. I still had acne and the need to be alluring when Ursula wouldn't look at me let alone touch me was important. Her name was Isobela and she didn't care I was married and neither did I. Ultimately I was alone. Didn't have the courage then to leave. Name that tune. It was not just a matter of courage; I felt I had to stand by her until we sold the house. I was flattered by the attention of the Italian and excited to meet a woman who had no qualms about being unfaithful to her husband. It was reassuring to have some laughter, some pleasure in life, no matter if it was wrong to betray Ursula. I wanted to live fully, as fully as the characters in the books I had read. I was gaining experience in the world and I knew the affair with Isobela would move me to act.

I met her at the Fellini festival at the Screen Cinema on D'Olier Street. She asked me for fire. I've heard Italians stop someone in the street since and ask for it and it sounds like practiced ignorance to beguile the natives but back then I didn't know a whole lot about anything. I told her she couldn't smoke in the cinema and she just smiled and wiggled her thumb in front of her cigarette as if it was a lighter and I lit it. I stared at the picture but wasn't able to concentrate. I could only be aware of her sitting beside me, smoking. After the picture was over we sat there while everyone else left and I turned and asked her out. We went across to what was then the Regency bar and had a drink. We gesticulated and laughed a lot. She was only three days in the country and had little English. She was reading *Ulysses* in Italian and when I told her it must be a hard book she didn't know what *hard* meant. I tapped the counter. Wood, she asked, raising her eyebrows. The way she raised her eyebrows, the charm of her befuddlement. She was flirting and making it clear she was flirting. She told me about her husband and somehow made it clear it was unimportant. She talked of him as if he was an aged relative. I couldn't talk of Ursula in the same way. I didn't want to talk of her at all. We went back

into the pictures and watched another Fellini. The lights went
down and she took my hand. My hand was sweating with nerves.
After a while she pulled my hand down between her legs but I
pulled it back. I couldn't do that, not here. She leaned over and
said something to me in Italian and kissed me. Her hand was
between my legs. Hard, she whispered, unzipping my trousers.
There is nothing to compare to a woman's knowing mouth. I will
take the memory of her lips to my grave.

I tried to write a story to make some meaning out of it. A young
man fantasises about being with a beautiful woman he sees on
the street. He takes the thought home with him and is rudely
interrupted by his bawling baby and frazzled wife, Ulrika (I
couldn't get away from the U). He doesn't have an affair. Instead
he helps his wife to soothe the child. He realises how he has
begun to look at his wife as a burden and how quickly they have
grown apart. They go to bed. He has a nightmare and wakes up
and realises the baby is screaming. In the last sentences of the
story he gets out of bed and goes to the child:

> I cradled our baby in my arms. "I'm so sorry," I whispered
> to her pudgy face. I brought her into the bedroom and sat
> beside Ulrika. Her face carried hours of exhaustion.
>
> "I love you," I said.
>
> She reached a hand out to mine and squeezed it. I stared
> at her, waiting. She said nothing.
>
> "Really, Ulrika. I love you."
>
> "Yes," she said.

What literature has lost. I was looking for some kind of understanding and forgiveness in the story I knew I would not find in
life, not that I understood why I was writing what I was writing
beyond the feeling of being trapped yet scared of freedom.
Looking for a truth in fiction to deny the lie in reality, perhaps.
In the midst of all this, Gerry phoned. He had emigrated to New
York. He was drunk. He had work for a good painter. Big money.
Ursula told me to take the opportunity but I didn't want to leave
her alone in the house. She laughed and said it would be different if it was the other way around. She wouldn't want to leave me
alone in the house. So I phoned Gerry and told him as soon as
the house was sold I would come over. My protestations about
staying were not honest. There was never any doubt that I would
go just as there was no doubt that she would leave town if an
assignment beckoned.

We are painting the house and can hear the music from the con-
cert in Lansdowne Road. I am rolling the ceiling and she is doing
the walls. I want it all to last as it was. With the cats and the roses
and the sun on the bed in the morning. The sleepy slosh of her
early morning piss. Driving her into the office. Letting her off in
Baggot Street at the *Turbine*. Kissing. There would always be one
last thing to say. I love you, I would say and she would smile a
gluttonous smile and slam the car door with the noise of Dublin
swirling around her. I would watch her in the quietness of the car.
I would stare after her, waiting for her to turn. I was caressed with
her through all the long day.

One morning, after I let her out at the corner, I see her wave to a man with a heavy duffel bag hanging off his shoulder. He is confident, easygoing. The way he carries himself. He smiles at her and she smiles back. The exchange flashes like a knife. She reaches into her briefcase and hands him a copy of her book. He shrugs and smiles at something she says and I sit there in the idling car wondering what she has to say to a man I don't know that could make him shrug and smile. He reads the blurb on the back of the book and hands it back. She bursts out laughing and slaps him on the arm. The horrible ease she has with him. Jealousy grips me and I have a stomach-churning insight of what she would feel if she found out about Isobela. You moral, Isobela said. We pray for Pope. We do not listen him.

I park the car and walk through Merrion Square, through the Lincoln Gate at Trinity, pass the chapel where Brefini and Medbh got married. They had said they would never marry—we listened to them rant about primitive Ireland, and then we watched them, as if in a surreal cartoon, marry and have Una and forget all the talk of changing the world. We had bought them a fridge that made its own ice cubes and they thanked us, missing our extravagant joke. Already their life was swallowed with baby burps and hoping the car would start in the morning. Getting married took the stress out of making the decision not to get married that they were making every day, Medbh said.

In the end I ran, not just from Ursula but from the crude trap of Dublin. The Tuesday before I left I told Medbh I was running. *Sometimes you need to run. Perhaps it's the only way to face your demon, we all have a demon, only one if we're lucky.* I can smell salt water when I think of what she said. Walking the pier in Irishtown. A boisterous day, the wind fighting with itself. Halfway down the pier, the heavens opened. We ran for the lighthouse.

I get up before Ursula. While I am waiting for the kettle to boil I walk out into the cold garden, Vomit and Willy bouncing about my feet. Full of meows and the happiness of morning. We have to let the little bastards out to empty their bladders—they still haven't worked out the cat flap. Rain during the night. Darkness loosening itself from a dirty sky. The absorbing silence of the city not yet awake. A bicycle squishes down the greasy hill. Then the dull plock of a tennis ball. They're starting early this year. The whack of a ball struck, the rattle of the protective wire between the end of the back garden and the courts. A ball lodged high up in one of the wire diamonds like an egg stuck in a startled mouth. A man's laughter from the tennis court. Willy scales to the top of the fencing to investigate. The kettle whistles and I go in and turn it off before it wakes her. Vomit sits on the builder's cement mixer, staring at her sister.

I blink with pleasure at the memory of her warm body, lost to sleep. Too early to wake her. I tap the foul-smelling cat food into the kittens' bowls and they race each other to their breakfast as I go to the toilet. Odd she never flushes. It smells of her. I gaze abstractly out the window as I urinate. The tennis players are rallying heavily. The man crashes a ball against the top of the net, curses and sets off to retrieve the ball that is marking his defeat. His partner takes off her tracksuit bottoms, flattens out the creases from her tennis skirt, and shakes off a chill. She hops on the spot, waiting. Aggression twitches in her calf. She embodies a certain kind of woman: a woman who dislikes men and, in return, is adored. They pursue her, searching for the nugget of her allure. I dislike everything her taut body suggests. My blood

rushes through me. I see myself lifting her tennis skirt and fucking her: a stiff penis has its own opinion. The idea of rape in
every man. The first day I met Ursula. The way I had to pull my
eyes away from her as she walked downstairs to the toilet in the
Palace Bar. The sway of her stout buttocks under a white skirt. I
felt naked in the pub, as if it was obvious that I was longing for
the impossible. I remember not liking her entirely. I drank deeply
then to steady the craving. The tennis ball thumps off the
asphalt. Have to get dressed. It's cold in the house. Tonight I'm
cooking. The future wouldn't happen. I want a child. The whack
of the ball off the tennis racket. But not with her. I open my eyes
and the world is too real, the way life always appears to be in the
midst of misery or ecstasy, as if it's happening to someone else.
The sky stares at me indifferently. Cognitive dissonance. The
presentation to the Japanese today. A child. The mirror stares at
my stupidity. The Japanese won't order, I know it, feel it in my
water. The mattress moans with her shift.

We are having dinner. She is eating salad noisily. It was when I
had begun to drink and had noticed it. Not so much that I
noticed it but that she had stopped drinking. It was her way of
telling me, of drawing attention to it. She had begun to know
me, knew the way my temper flared with the breeze of her per-
ceptiveness and so she said no, she would have no wine. For a
while I cut back but then I weakened to opening a bottle at the
end of the meal, then would rouse myself just before we started
the salad. Finally I was reduced to glassfuls while we finished eating. During that dinner it's obvious the marriage is slipping. It's

like the L on her typewriter that can't bring itself to strike paper
hard enough to make an impression. The harder the key is struck
the fainter its outline. I wash back the anger; it swims in my ears.
I stare out the window at the tarmac drive that runs up to the
edge of the window. It's always a shock to see the neighbour cut
through the garden, her frail feet passing by at eye level. I
breathe deeply and imagine her eating becoming sweet music.
She must have always eaten that way. I get up abruptly from the
table and leave the room to steady myself. She shouts after me.
Do I want tea. Her voice eddies on the waves of anger I leave
behind. The air is a favourite cup, broken. I come in after an
hour's walk and there is a mug of tea on the table with a saucer
over it to keep it warm.

The smell of our sweat lost its passion. She no longer liked my
smell about her nostrils. It all slipped between our hands. It was
a long time happening (weeks, months, years?) but now it seems
as fast as losing sight of a fish flipping in a river.

August: Summer trying to break out of a wet July. We are tiling
in the bathroom upstairs. The telephone rings, we look at each
other, at our hands covered in tiling cement. It's Friday evening.
Invariably the paper rings on Friday evening. Looking for her to
go to Leopardstown to cover a race meeting. She must have been
first on the list; the freelancer who drops her life in the sink to ask
rich men stupid questions.

—Leave it.

She is wiping her hands clean.

—It might be the office.

—The office is why I don't want you to pick it up.

The answering machine clicks on downstairs. Isobela's voice. I make a U on the back of the tile and wipe it clean. The Italian voice is a fired gun to my ears. Ursula looks at me for an instant and I see suspicion coming into her eyes. She goes into the study next door, picks up the extension, and says hello and calmly, so calmly it startles me, Isobela says hello and asks if she may speak to her friend, Stephen. Stee-pen. I sit in the bath, staring at the half-finished wall listening to their voices echo up the stairs from the machine. Ursula puts the phone down and comes back in. I talk out of nervousness.

—Put the lid on the cement or it'll harden.

I pick up the phone and my hello is the voice of the accused.

—Hi, Lover.

Isobela's voice is a warm crumpled bedsheet. Life is falling away. I tell her I am busy doing the bathroom and make a joke about her voice echoing around the house as we speak. Guilt stiffens me. She talks about going back to Italy soon—I interrupt and tell her I'm going to New York. Her voice is assured and friendly. She brings the conversation to a silky end. Women are better liars. I put the phone down and wipe a smudge of cement off it. The courts are full now with Friday evening tennis players, ready to bash the week out of their minds. Lover.

Ursula is washing herself at the bathroom sink, naked except for white knickers and flat black shoes. Her overalls lie on the windowsill. The knicker elastic is cutting into her flesh; the hairs on her legs standing with the cold.

—They can see you from here.

—Who?

—The tennis players.

—Big thrill.

She dresses and does herself up. She closes the hall door quietly when she leaves. The clutch grinds as she reverses out the drive. I stand in the hallway surrounded by the tremendous silence of her leaving. A moment later the doorbell rings. A couple of children stand in the porch, red-faced and breathless:

—Can we have our ball back, mister?

They step inside to wait. I go out into the back and search for it. Willy and Vomit are fighting on the grass.

—Where is it? Where's the ball, girls?

The voice that comes out of my mouth is calm. I get the DART into town and go into Scanlon's. Three morose pints. Two men arguing at the bar. *It is. I'm telling you it is. You know what your problem is. I'll tell you what your problem is. You don't know what the fuck you're talking about—that's your problem.* I walk home in the rain, enjoying that pathetic fallacy of it all without an umbrella. The phone is ringing when I get to the front door. She's probably gone to her mother's to bitch and that cunt has filled her with superwoman confidence about her life. I pick up the phone and say hello as dourly as possible. It's Gerry, telling me it's now or never. Shit or get off the pot he says. I hate that phrase. Ursula doesn't come home that night and she doesn't phone. I wake up, feed her cats (already the dividing up—it floods in unbidden) and stare out at the rain dripping off the gutter. Fuck it. Fuck her. Fuck whatever anyone thinks. I walk into town and buy the ticket to New York. I walk back as if in a parade, wanting to be on view to the world with my new resolve. That night I root the television out of its box and plug it in. I sit watching it but I'm only waiting for her to phone. Every hour that passes and she doesn't phone is an hour more to tell myself I'm right in going. I hate that I need her to push me into a decision but sitting there I know this is the way I am. I leave the television on so the locals think someone is in and go to the pub for a bottle of whiskey. No messages on the machine when I get back. I pour a drink and the phone rings. Isobela saying she's going tomorrow, looking for a lift to the airport. I tell her my wife has left me and there's no car. Poor baby, she says, from two women to no women. I tell her I'll get a bus out with her. Bus, she says, with disgust. Taxi. I get taxi. Get taxi then, I say. We both laugh and say goodbye. Come visit she says. No, I say. Okay Irish, she says. Be happy. I tell her I'll write to her from New York.

Two more days pass and no sign from her. If she expects me to phone her she can go to hell. She did the walking out. Come Saturday whether she's there or not I'm going. The cats can starve. I sleep little on the Friday night, cursing her. I was sure she'd be home by the weekend. The cats wake me meowing at the bedroom door. I feed them, take my suitcases down to the hall and walk around the house one last time. The note is on the kitchen table. *It's going to take some time. I need a break. I'd take the cats but you know they hate being moved. I'll be in touch.* It's a strange feeling, realising she had been in the house while I was sleeping, in and out like a thief. Need some time. I'll give you time baby. I call Medbh, and Brefini answers. I ask them to pass on a message to her. After I put the phone down I realise how forced my voice was, controlled and clipped. That it has come to this, a terse message through friends.

New York

New York, New York. Life exploding. Hot dog stands, pretzels, bagels, rocketing subways, yellow cabs, jazz 24/7 on the radio, Liza Minnelli advertised the length of a bus, summer thunderstorms, the ricochet of strange languages on street corners. In New York my eyes opened and I realised how insane our life had become. I felt safe there and hated the house in Dublin and hated what had happened to our life. I hated it ending, the years of compromising to make it work coming to nothing.

My first job is painting a gallery in Commerce Street in the Village. I work long hours, not just to make a good impression but to avoid going out. New York intimidates me. There are too many choices. In a foreign city everyone seems to have a purpose. And of course I work to avoid calling her. I dwell on things

that I had pushed aside in more generous moments: her visible
envy when I was promoted to line leader and then manager. She
is incapable of enjoying success, either mine or her own. The
Ambitious enjoy nothing, always one step behind the next goal.
She is a somewhat successful writer now and her competitiveness
baffles and disgusts me. Time magnifies faults.

I worry about the cats even though I know she would have been
over to them in a shot. I telephone her. She thanks me for looking after the cats and for phoning Medbh. She's glad I'm doing
something to change and I bite my tongue, wanting to tell her
what to do with her patronising insights. A frightening distance
between us, lengthened by civility. There would be more passion
if we were enemies. She tells me to hang in there and enjoy New
York. Everything is fine in Soapy Avenue. Wimbledon is on and
the children are playing tennis rather than football. She isn't in the
house often, she is too busy with work. She tells me a letter is in
the post—one to forget. Here beats the harsh heart of truth. It is
possible to lie to Ursula, and later to lie to Holfy, even possible to
lie to myself that the relationship is over, but untruthful words on
the page mock everything that goes before and everything that
follows. The lie destroys a story as surely as it destroys trust
between people. It demotes everything to fiction.

The letter to forget:

> Happy Birthday. I loved the doll, loved it. I miss you.
> You don't miss me. You're not with me. Not because you
> are there but because you are not with me in your head.
> It's not my imagination. I'm losing you. Shit. I never

thought I'd be coming out with this kind of nonsense. You
are not thinking about us. I can feel you not thinking
about us. What's happening? Tell me. Just tell me.

My mother is still with Mulvany. I'll have to stop calling
him that or I'll actually refer to him that way in his
presence. I was dropping some cakes in the other day and I
let myself into the house. Nine o'clock in the morning and
the television was blaring. He was lying on the floor with
the dog, licking his balls. He was licking the dog's balls.
Can you imagine what goes on in a mind that would do
such a thing? What can I say to her? I love her. She'll
only—I know what you'll say and you're right, but it's so
complicated. She sucks solace from him. He makes her feel
young and pretty. You bastard. I couldn't say it to your
face—I knew you were so thrilled to get out of here. But to
go now? You know I didn't want you to go. And you know I
would never tell you not to go. Can't you make a visit back
before Christmas? Is this really going to make such a
difference in money? Not really. ~~Certainly not for us.~~

I'm inundated with work. Fiona wants me to do
something about babies. A sweet milkybreathed piece.
Maybe even a series of three. You know what'd be good,
Urs, she says to me. I always know she's taking advantage
of me when she calls me that. Can you believe the woman?
After four years freelancing for her she's going to give me
my first series on nappy changing. Feminism, roll over and
die. I shouldn't complain. She does seem genuinely
interested in me, at least as long as I'm standing in front of
her. Fuck it—At least she's cutting me slack on deadlines.

I miss you.

Is Manhattan cold? Tell me where you eat. Let me live
it with you a little. Kiss. Need a real one though.

Urs-ula

Dearest Ursula,
New York?

*

*

*

*

*

*

*

*

*

*

*

*

*

*

*

*

*

*

*

*

*

*

*

It's snowing.
    S.

My anger at that time, anger fueled by her instinct for knowing. Phoning her to reassure her. Angry that she sensed what I was going to do before I even did it. Women know these things, Isobela had said. Women know these things. I hate that women-power shit. But then another letter, softer, on yellow lined paper:

She was arrested. She was running down St. Kevin's Avenue, naked except for her white tights, screaming Where's my pussy? Where's my pussy? The dog was missing too. And the German silverware Gran gave her as a wedding present. No sign of her beau. She had drunk three bottles of Bailey's. No wonder she's putting on weight. There's no point in telling Daddy. He'll only gloat.

I can't believe you still have all that snow. Even though it sounds awful, it must be fun. Anything would be a change from this rain. Cecil and his team haven't showed up since last Tuesday. Everything they say about builders is not true. They're much worse.

I'm doing an article on fidelity (read infidelity). About our parents' generation. The men were so nice. They talked to me as if I was an understanding daughter. They disgusted me with their stories of love. This face of mine: Empathy personified you called it once. It's a good article. Punchy and moving. The kind Fiona likes. Trevor liked it, she told me. Who's Trevor, says I. Trevor owns the paper, says she, searching my face for journalistic prowess. I only know him as Mr. Plausible. It's in Sunday's. Veronica has an article below mine—The Irish Illiterati. 1500 words on the new wave of publishing in this country. Between herself and myself we make for a thrilling page. You want to see her since they offered her a contract—flouncing into the office with the hair bobbing off her shoulders. If only she kept her crotch as clean as her golden locks.

Medbh's baby is due in two weeks. Send her something nice. I don't think Brefini wanted this right now.

Keep biting the Apple.

Ursula

PS: You shouldn't keep buying the paper. Although you're right—it's worth five dollars to read me.

PPS: It's wicked to be alone in our bed although there is a masochistic pleasure in the wait for you. I lie on my hand and imagine it's yours. You've a wonderful hand. The pleasure it gives. But you know that. I can feed on the waiting. Let's work something out. We can, I'm sure. Daisies are my favourite flowers. It's the size of them. They understand each other's tininess. Nothing, not even a daisy, is as beautiful as the love we once had. Kiss.

Leaving Bath Avenue

I go back to Dublin the day before the auction. I am even more
determined to leave. Already I am feeling like a foreigner. My
heart sinks when I arrive at the house. It does look beautiful. I
have no inkling how to broach ending.

We are in the garden and planting sunflowers because Ruth
likes them so much. Ursula is clearing the bindweed that is chok-
ing the roses. There is a thud and the sound of running. A dead
cat lies on the grass. She doesn't hear it. I lift the animal and
throw it back over the wall before she turns. We go to a film that
evening. When we get back the children are in the front garden
ripping up the flowers. I keep driving and we go to the Beggars
Bush and sit in silence, drinking. It is a public admission of

defeat. I am full of rage at the neighbours—not the ones who cause trouble, the ones who don't—the friendly neighbours who know what's happening and do nothing to help. I despise these people who call themselves friends. Grand morning. Sure you have it looking lovely. If there's anything I can do. They do worse than nothing. Their refusal to acknowledge our torment is the loudest comment of all that there is no community in this place that prides itself on its friendliness. The Good Old Dubs. That night Ursula asks me if I would mind if she dedicates *Womb* to her grand-aunt instead of to me as she had intended. Dedicate the poems to the old woman who might not live much longer. I think of the work I had put into the poems with her; the close reading verse by tedious verse, the arguing for hours over whether to use this word or that, whether or not this poem is strong enough to be included, the careful arranging of the order of the poems, and the endless encouragement to send them out. I do not care to tell her how much the dedication means to me. If she does not know, there is no point in telling her. What difference would it make? She might dedicate it to me and then the old bitch would kick the bucket. Or she will dedicate it to Edith anyway as she does in the end. What does it matter how I feel? What matters is how she feels—the old wrinkled lesbian matters more. What my father said to me the night before I married: Remember, blood is blood. I had misunderstood him.

Edith had never married. Men were like horses, Edith had said, beautiful but too much trouble to bother with. Ursula felt a kinship with this woman and admired the life she had led. She thought I was generous to tell her to go ahead and dedicate the book to Edith. Hurt pride appearing as an act of generosity. After

Womb comes out, I feel a final release from her through the one thing that has kept us together for so long: poetry. A poem she did not show me before publication. A poem about Ruth's illness when she was given the wrong drugs and her body went rigid. Nothing could be done except to wait until the effect wore off. It was one of the last times that Ursula saw Ruth alive and she was horrified to see her in such a state. There it was: my sister's pain shaped in a few mediocre Anglo-Irish lines. The only difference between poets and prostitutes is that poets work for less money.

Despite all the disparities, all the flaws, we still liked each other and wanted to be together. Even after we agreed to end it all I still dreamed of living with her in an old house overlooking the sea. Nothing but the sound of birds landing and scurrying on the flat roof over our heads. After the sale of the house on Bath Avenue—even before it—we could move into An Tigh Bocht in Dalkey and renovate, and then we would never have to worry about money again. We were young and we could work it out.

And this is what we did, at least for a while. We worked day and night, finishing Bath Avenue and starting Dalkey. I remember painting the hall door of the house in Dalkey the same yolk yellow I had painted the hall door in Bath Avenue while Ursula was giving a radio interview. It was raining lightly and I was proud, listening to her defend her view from some obnoxious chat-show host who played the intellectual. The painted door would be a nice surprise for her. We would start a new garden here. *We.* I was carried away with myself and denying the truth. New York had taken hold of me. I wanted to go back, to go home, because for the first time in my life, *somewhere* felt like home. What I also denied was that I wanted to go alone.

The final frightening moment in Bath Avenue. The first day
that the house is on view. The market is buoyant and we know
we will be swamped with viewers. An hour before the viewing, a
gang gathers at the corner. We sit in the kitchen on one side of
the beautifully damp-proofed, beautifully papered, beautifully
painted wall, and they sit on the other side, smoking cigarettes.
They don't do anything. They don't have to do anything. No
one will buy. Already cars are pulling up. It is no use calling the
Gardaí. The sight of a squad car will only make matters worse.
We hold each other. It is the first time in months we touch. The
softness of her against me. That time on our honeymoon. The
estate agent comes and we leave the house. The house doesn't
sell at auction.

An Tigh Bocht

We have begun a life in Dalkey and now panic grips me. Bath Avenue is still not sold and I promised I would stay until the sale comes through. I am falling in love with this new place. We have slipped into working on the house and it's work we know well. We laugh about learning from old mistakes (meaning tiling and dry rot, she says, killing the joke). We don't talk about ourselves, falling into bed each night too tired for sex to be a problem anymore.

The estate agent phones to say we have an offer on Bath Avenue, five thousand under our minimum and Ursula says take it. *Just tell her now. Just say it's over. This is it.* We go out to celebrate and I say nothing.

We are driving home from *A Dry White Season*, a film about a white man's attempt to end apartheid in South Africa. He succeeds

a little but dies in the attempt. I start to cry behind the wheel of
the car. Ursula asks me to pull over. I am embarrassed that she is
seeing me crying, and I keep driving. Through my convulsions I
tell her how unbearable life is, that Ruth is dead and dead goes
on and on, that people kill each other for absurd reasons. I laugh
at how hollow words sound. We are stopped at a traffic light on
the Blackrock Road and I tell her what I have wanted to tell her
for a long time, that it is over and we cannot go on, that whatever
has happened is irreparable. I am stunned with my own words,
now that the house on Bath Avenue is sold and we are moving
into Dalkey; now that all the horror of what we have been
through is finished. Yes, she says and with her yes we are buoyed
with relief and begin to talk like old friends, talk as if we are a
mature couple looking back on a younger, more naïve pair. We
are talking about different people, old selves, dead love battered
and choked with the pull of life. She tells me she wants to have a
child, has wanted to for some time now, but could not bring herself to say it. It had come on her out of the blue and frightened her.

The unspoken drove us apart. From the moment we met we
had both passionately agreed there would be no children. I
sensed it before she did. It was in her poems. Female loss. Female
strength. Female rage. Emptiness. Nesting. Writing perhaps is a
way of asking the questions when the answers are already breathing. It's easy to see now the reason why we didn't discuss it. It was
a problem that had no room for compromise. By her thirty-
second birthday she was silently frantic.

Children. You never know what it's going to be like, they say.
You have no idea how your life changes. Everything revolves
around them. How tired I grow of all the talk. I have listened to

people all my life tell me how lucky I am to have the freedom of
not having them. What an endless burden it is having them
always. They have no idea, these parents, the endless burden in
not having children. I am sick of the used wrapping of people's
lives strewn on the floor. Sometimes it's as if the only choice is
whether or not to have children.

My mind was soaking up the things I would miss: the clematis
had not flowered the first year I planted it. It had almost died that
first winter but it hung weakly to the trellis, and I was certain it
would bloom this year. The roses, too, were slow in catching,
and had to be protected from Vomit and Willy who loved their
soil. Love is buried in many ways.

We fight one night over who cooks dinner and she yells that
it's her damn house and I look at her with a coldness, an aloofness
that is new to me. I feel no compassion for her. I walk to my
father's house and move in with him.

I pack what is clearly mine and stack the white boxes in a corner of the garage in Dalkey. My greatest concern is that the
books will curdle in the dampness. We argue over who owns
what. It is not a selfish battle. We fight with generosity, each
insisting the other has more need or claim to the kettle, the print,
the vacuum cleaner, the shared desk. Our generosity is in truth
anything but. I use generosity to show her it is ending because of
her selfish needs and partly to assuage my own guilt over the
affairs that she has not discovered (I learned once one affair is
started the language of deceit is the easiest language of all to
speak). I want then to show myself to be her moral superior.
When it ends, it is me who leaves the house. It is, after all, her
home. It is hard for her middle-class ego to bear the idea of

throwing the working-class sweetheart out onto the street. This is why it is me who speaks the words that bring our end, words spoken not out of courage, but desperation.

The division of friends. It hits me like a tree falling that the friends I have were made through Ursula. Some people make an effort to stay in touch with me but finally their allegiance asserts itself in an unringing telephone. Ursula wants to settle. Settle. A word carrying the weight of unborn children.

My father is reading something out of the paper about Northern Ireland, repeating what he always repeats. *Should get a chain saw and divide North and South and let them float off into the Atlantic.* I stop listening to him and realise how much I am losing in Dublin: the late nights in bed together reading favourite worst passages from the books Ursula was reviewing, the walks on Dalkey hill, playing with the cats, pruning roses, sitting in a pub on a Saturday night, planning. All these things weaken my resolve and I telephone Ursula the day before I am due to leave for New York again. She agrees to meet me in Caviston's.

She laughs at the change in my ordering—I am always awkward in ordering, feeling I might be asked to leave before I even get to the table. But now I call the waitress over and ask for some water before I even order. The sophisticate. To my surprise the waitress brings the water. I question the waitress about the menu and I do it not to impress Ursula (although I would have if it made any difference) but because anger is the only thing that pushes me to assertion. We order wine but I can hardly drink it because of my nerves and I blurt out that we should try again, here or even in New York. Before she opens her mouth I know what she will say. I can see it in her eyes, see her reach for the words that will not hurt, and when she does say no, when she explains that whatever it was that bonded us is gone, and she feels nothing for me, not even anger, when she says these words I hardly hear her. I am riveted by her face. Her expression is one I have never known. She has a calmness and resoluteness that makes her a stranger. It is the face of a person in complete control. The pain I see in her eyes is not for the loss of what we once had but rather for the humiliating position I have put myself in, and the hopelessly awkward position I have put her in, sitting here in front of this well-chosen meal. She is far beyond me. The worst aspect of the evening is listening to her soften the blow and at the same time thread carefully so she will say nothing to offer any encouragement. Her tone is laden with the kindness offered a stranger who has tripped and fallen in the street.

I curse myself for not waiting until the end of the meal. Now, we have to go through the farce of eating as if nothing has happened. I consider leaving, but pride keeps me in my seat. I even order dessert and joke with the waitress. Ursula tells me stories about the newspaper, stories about petty journalists and pettier editors. She has discovered that Wheatley, whose work we both detest, had indeed slept her way into the job. There would have been a time when that outraged Ursula but I can tell from her voice that it shocks her no more. Why do people begin to become the people you want them to be when it's too late? She tells me too, in the only intimate moment she shares, that she still wants a child. She was shopping last week, she says, and she saw a beautiful child in a pram and she could understand how women are moved to steal babies. We finish our tea and step out into separate nights.

She offers me a lift back into town but I decline. She offers again and I say yes, still not wanting to appear hurt. As we drive

in along the coast road I look across the Strand at Sandymount, at
a late-night rider cantering along the sand near the edge of the
ebbing tide, and beyond the Strand there is Dollymount beach
where my father took Ruth and me with soggy tomato sandwiches when we were children, all of it fading now under the
darkening sky, and as the city grows closer I force myself not to
look in the direction of Bath Avenue as we head for the North-
side. She is making conversation and I try to enter into it but am
tired. Words separate us now. Words weave in and out like cor-
dons. It takes forever to say anything that matters. Words are big
and clumsy with us; they spill out failures. The things that have
shaped our lives. The white trousers she wore that evening. The
slope of her breasts beneath the blouse as she talked about Win-
nicot. I am tired of Dublin, of trying to make sense of my life here,
tired of Ruth's death, and as we cross the Liffey together for the
last time it sinks into me that she is right: it is over. I am tired of
her. I look at her hand on the steering wheel. If she were a colour
she would be beige. I smile to myself at the cold boredom I feel
towards her. For the first time in our life together, I let myself feel
indignant in her presence and I think of a last parting shot. I think
of all the times I did not retaliate in arguments and now I want her
to remember the last words I will ever utter to her. I will cut her
down just as I am getting out of the car and then close the door
before she has a chance to answer. She pulls up outside my father's
house and she turns off the engine. I look at her. Maybe she too
has a parting shot. But it is not in me to do it. I can almost hear
Ruth whisper: Not worth it. No bitterness. Go the other road.

I will go back to New York. I will find something there. Something will happen. I haven't let go of Ursula but I will. One day I
will show her the indifference she feels for me now.

᠅   ᠅   ᠅

I cannot even remember the sound of my sister's voice. It is gone.
Her voice has become a huge silence. I loved her laughter but I
can only remember that her laugh provoked laughter in me. Her
sweet contagious music is gone. There is only the photograph of
her gesticulating with the fork and the roaring silence of the
page in front of me. The rest is words hobbling after indistinct
memories. The true nightmare of death is forgetting. I forget
Ruth, she who I believe I loved more than anyone. Knowing that
I have forgotten much of what Ruth was, knowing I too will be
forgotten. This is the face of survival. It does away with the fallacy of a pure, everlasting love between human beings. But there
was the evening in the kitchen in the flat in Dun Laoghaire. I was
sitting trying to meditate and wanting Ruth with me, wanting
her back. The sound of the fridge in the corner was distracting
me and I had almost decided to give up. Relaxed, open concentration alluded me. I got up, unplugged the fridge, and the room
fell into silence. I looked out the window at two crows fighting
with each other at the end of the garden. The sound of their
squawking audible, even behind the glass. My mind cleared and
there was nothing—that splendid moment that is akin to the hia-
tus that stretches between orgasm and sleep. Orgasm, that
release from the self, and meditation the enclosure of the self.
Ruth was there, before me. Her essence. A calmness as if nothing
else existed. The same sensation of watching a film where an
actor leaves the room and the camera doesn't follow and yet the
essence lingers in the full stillness of the moment. I felt her presence grow, then, and I felt happiness emanate from her and dumb
fear gripped me in my gut and she was gone. I sat there, sweating

and feeling as if there was a shard of ice stuck in my stomach. Sins became harder to live with.

I became intensely infatuated with the women I slept with while I was with Ursula, but I knew it was not love. I thought it was passionate lovemaking but it was nothing as calculated as that. I was getting over the problem I had had for years with her. I was trying to satisfy that pent-up sexual hunger that could not be satisfied. The heat of the sex was the one area of life where I was not acting. It was a desire to live, as if my own life was running out quickly, the way Ruth's had. I heard a psychologist on the radio talk about near-death experiences and how these make people change, how they reassess their lives, improve them. She was talking theory. That's the problem with psychologists and priests. It's always theory. Some evenings on the way home from work, or from the hospital, I would slip my seat belt off and drive faster and faster, imagining that it would be all over shortly. There was no fear in me of death, only a fear of the endless pain. But I would think of Ruth hearing of the news of my death and I would slow down and go and visit one of the women who I knew would have me. I poured all of myself into these women, all the longing and ache of life. As I lay in bed, I could tell they knew they were soothing what was locked inside me and I was embarrassed. I would never fall asleep until I was certain the woman was as drained as I was, sure she had come no matter how much sleep pulled me. I needed the mutual exhaustion. I had no expectations of these women, and, more importantly, they had none of me. There were no expectations at all except the pleasure of the moment. Until Holfy.

H o l f y

She can only be described through her city. Even more specifi-
cally: Gansevoort Street. Melville walked this street here in the
far West Village in New York City. The author of *Moby Dick*
found it hard to get work on a street named after his relatives.
Holfy took on Gansevoort Street in the early sixties. Stonewall
was years away from her, and I was not yet born.

She gets bored easily. In 1974 she started a restaurant with her
then lover in the heart of Greenwich Village. The Black Man's
Table still does well almost a quarter of a century later in a city
that devours restaurants before the paint has dried on their
freshly finished fronts. But the restaurant bored her, she had a
disagreement with her lover, and she left. Success in itself seems

as uninteresting to her as the same meal two nights in a row. Then she got herself into photography in a city lit by photographers.

Holfy started buying her own train tickets from upstate New York to Manhattan as soon as she was old enough. At eighteen she flew to Denmark and took painting classes. She would become a painter. She sat on both sides of the canvas. Life opened. A year later, when she returned to New York, she and Robert rented a dump on Gansevoort Street in the guts of New York's meat district. They knocked down the wall between them and the adjoining vacant apartment. When the landlord found out, there was nothing he could do because the lease stated *Apartment, second floor.* There was nothing describing another apartment on that floor in the plans. It was fun in those days to fool the landlord. Like his tenants, Charlie Gottleib was young and vigorous.

At night, on Little West Twelfth Street, a sliver of a block from her doorway, prostitutes prance on the cobblestone roads that have been battered by Mack trucks delivering skirts of beef to New York's finest restaurants. In the filthy night, these prostitutes glisten, looking more outrageously beautiful than supermodels and with smoother legs. On a summer's evening, even before darkness gives the hookers mystery, cars stalk the area. Syringes litter the streets on Sunday mornings. A prostitute is slumped in a doorway, his silver miniskirt gathered on his hips. The smell of urine teases the breeze that wafts in from the Hudson River. It is quiet.

During the week, Duffy Dumpster trucks collect the rubbish. Other trucking companies collect the inedible meat refuse after eleven at night. The meat is sprayed with green dye to discourage the homeless from eating it. Bins, as large as small apartments, crash to the ground throughout the night as they are emptied. No sooner has the rubbish been collected than the meat deliveries turn into the street. They park every which way, engines coughing. When the drivers are blocked they rest their elbows on their horns until someone moves. By five, the hour between night and morning, the workers arrive. They scream at each other in Aramaic and Spanish. Someone speaks English. Holfy sleeps with her windows open to the mouth of the street.

She has made her home here for over thirty years. During the summer she cycles to her appointments on her bokety bicycle, bouncing over the broken cobblestones and splashing through rivulets of blood that run out of the processing plants. If she's out, the mailman drops off her photography packages at Florent's restaurant next door. On the hottest days the stench seems visible and during snowy winter mornings the street is an abstract painting—Jackson Pollock playing with colours. I am entranced with it all but it wears off, although in the company of a woman like Holfy the excitement of living never fades.

Her studio is in this apartment. It is packed densely with contact sheets, negatives, photography books, film books, novels, poetry, jazz, classical, clothes, shoes, makeup, and light; the light she gained thirty years ago when she knocked down that wall. These days she feels guilty about the wall. Charlie never did well in the meat business. Soon, in his late sixties, he will break down and end up in an asylum. Photographs of old lovers are pasted on her walls. There are photographs of Robert in the last days of his illness. For her, it's an expression of love, a visual depiction of how much he grew as he died. For me, it's a macabre showing of decay, a photographic equivalent of Lucian Freud. His ghost lives here. Many of the photographs are of naked men, their nudity compounded and not neutralised by their number. She photographs her friends for pleasure. She is in pursuit of an aspect of the personality they seldom display. She shoots quickly and seductively. She takes chances. She spends ages taping gels on her strobes and then doesn't use them. She is restless when she works and yet somehow she captures most of her subjects in a state of tranquillity.

The first time I laid eyes on her she was shooting at the IBM kick-off. That was before I learned that I could be dishonest and live with fickleness. Fickle. That was the kind of word Holfy used. Fickle, and credible. Credible was her most condescending term.

I was still staying with Gerry that first night I met her in the Puck Building. Gerry had been giving me the hint that I'd have to get my own place. IBM had won the Cunard account. Gerry had worked with Fintan, the guy who gave us both under-the-table work, and Fintan had worked with Cunard and got us an invite. She is crouching at my table taking photographs of the marketing director while he gives his lighthearted nautical speech. Gerry and I laugh, not at his speech but at his tic—constantly lifting his chin away from his collar as if the shirt is tweaking his neck. A finger taps my shoulder.

—That's Mr. Welty?

She's pointing her middle finger at the podium. I smile a yes at her. She finishes her roll, replaces it, writes something on the spent roll, and slips it into a fanny pack. I watch her working for the rest of the evening. She has a precise economy of movement as she works the hall. I think about talking to her and then dismiss her—as one does with these idiosyncratic New York types. But I remembered that middle finger pointing.

Months later I am at the Gay Men's Health Crisis benefit on Christopher Street. I forget now what I was doing there. Something altruistic. I was with William Davies. We had painted Bill's gallery, and Bill was after Gerry. There she was photographing again. No sleek black suit this time. An official Keith Haring T-shirt with green shorts. She is laughing a lot. She seems to know a lot of the people she is photographing. She touches them gently on the arm, pushing them into poses. Someone hands her a glass of wine, which she takes and then leaves on the sidewalk. Bill and I are sitting on an overturned barrel at the end of Christopher. The cops are relaxing, laughing at a drunken Judy Garland look-alike whimper that he isn't in Kansas anymore. Bill is watching me watch her.

—You like her?

—Who?

—Holmfridur. The photographer.

—You know her?

—Sure. The one and only Holmfridur Olafsdottir.

—Holmwho?

—Holmfridur Olafsdottir. Imagine crunching your teeth. She's a fag hag.

She has her hair in a ponytail.

Holmfridur, he says again, smiling. He wants me to appear a little stupid, never missing the edge knowledge gives. He gets up with his half-eaten chicken drumstick and goes over to her. She responds much more warmly than he expects. Not the usual strained friendliness that trails Bill's sick life.

—I'm Holfy, she says, giving me the gift of her hand. Long fingers. She speaks as if she has marbles in her mouth. She doesn't remember me.

—We met—talked—at the IBM thing a few months back. At the Puck?

—Right. I remember.

She doesn't.

—You asked me the name of some guy.

Her face darkens. She remembers.

—You're the fuckhead who lost me the account?

—I beg your pardon?

—You said Welty was the M.D. and he wasn't.

—I was just joking. I thought you knew I didn't know any of those gobshites.

—Expensive joke.

She walks off.

—O, dear, you do have a way with women.

—Want to do it Bill?

He looks at me quickly to see if I mean it. He's imagining pushing me down on my stomach but already I am walking after her.

—I love this garlic chicken, she says to some wrinkled queen, stripping a morsel from the bone and popping it in her mouth.

—I'll pay.

She looks around at me.

—I'll pay for whatever I cost you.

—Fifty thousand.

I pale and the queen laughs.

—It was five thousand, and future business.

—I'll pay the five. I can't get the business back.

—You'll pay the five?

Earnest nod.

—Okay. Send the check here.

I take the card and walk down Christopher Street. I walk across to Washington Square, whistling. Then I think of the money. Lot of money for a phone number. That was the beginning of life with her.

I'm as sick of Gerry as he is of me. His girlfriend is some Jew with the classic honker who makes furniture out of sheet metal. He's either too dumb or too indifferent to be bothered by her fake orgasms but it's getting to me. I've put the word out to everyone I meet that I need something. The response is always the same. Everyone is always looking for a place. Every day there is always someone shouting in the window of the gallery wanting to know if it is being renovated into an apartment.

I start to pick up books again but it seems meaningless. Cynical voices. People who have nothing to say, saying their nothing with glossy panache. I begin to walk the streets a lot. In the evening I turn on the radio. The same voices discussing the same problems. I feel cold and put on my old jacket. Rummage for a cigarette. The letter that arrived yesterday that I was afraid to open. I had written in weakness and asked her to reconsider, to say yes. I find it in the inside pocket and open it. I feel shame rise as I read it. She is right.

> What you say you want. What you need. I need to
> explore myself. I can't believe you're coming out with that
> shit. Are you looking for my blessing? Why don't you just

say it? You want to fuck around. You don't have the balls
to say it. You want to go and search for the balls you don't
have. You know who you should fuck? Yourself. And you
know nothing of my passions. You are an assumption with
a steady voice. You have become plausible. You sound like
Brefini. He talks nonstop about how wonderful Una is and
he wouldn't change a nappy if shit was coming out her
shoes. Shit smells so men like him—and you— take notice.

I am solid. Dependable. This is what you prefer to
think. You pour stoicism into me. One thing I do know
about us is that I got to know you well and you got to
know me not at all. I am a mystery to myself—how can
you claim to know me? This is not aphoristic babble—the
kind you excel in uncurling at dinner parties. This is the
truth. As for your honesty? Fuck your honesty. I wanted
commitment.

You started listening less. Surely one needs to listen
more as the mystery of two lives deepens. It's harder to
see what is already there. I can remember the month you
stopped trying: the weary and contented roll away from
me and the snoring. You can only be yourself through
your work, you say. Such indulgent twaddle. I was always
with you. Never for a moment did my mind stray from
you—from us. What do words say, you ask. What do
words say. Words are no proof. Actions are proof, you
say. So you went into management for us? So you wore
those suits for me? So you ate in the Orchid Szechwan
every second day for me? So you went to New York for
me. Proof is what I do not need, thank you. Proof is an
ending. I was looking—I am looking—for a continuum.

Once I knew you; at your beginning; learning you like
a petal learning sunshine. My hand on the smooth

trembling of your desire. Such tenderness in the intensity
of your restraint. You waited for me then. Love was in the
containment of your release. Your fingers held the
moment of my pleasure. You opened me to the pleasure of
myself: my ankle surprised by the kisses of your lips.
Finding excitement on the tips of my fingers. Afterwards,
your flaccidness resting against me like a tongue. Your
hand bringing me to climax. How that hand made me
come. An hour later I could feel my uterus tightening and
loosening.

You didn't leave me in January. You left me a long time
ago. Long before New York. You abandoned me when our
minds conceived each other as a single entity.
Abandoned: cruel, forlorn word. The tears won't stop. I
can't believe I'm this weak. I never liked the way you
whispered obscenities in my ear during lovemaking. I
should have told you that long ago. I kept too much to
myself. Mea culpa. Mea culpa no more. I'm telling people
why you deserted. Is deserted too strong? Pick a word. I
do think it would be inappropriate for me to be the bearer
of your morality. We don't want to shroud our lives in lies.
Do we?

The darling wife, Ursula.

Remember. Every time you piss. Every time you put it
in someone. Take a look at it and remember your wife.

We are in the downtown Guggenheim to see some modern art.
She is educating me although she would deny such a grand
claim. We are in front of an Agnes Martin, a blank canvas. The
museum is empty save for us and the attendant. Holfy is talking
about the artist's life. I try to hide boredom, irritation at this pre-

tentious canvas. I say nothing because my comments seem so ordinary, so commonplace they embarrass me. There is too much of my father in me to be taken in by this kind of art. How many bags of potatoes would that buy, he'd say. Holfy is talking about the artist's spirituality. Her depth and commitment to statement. As I stare at the canvas, thin grey lines emerge. There is a grid system as clear as a map of Manhattan itself. Lines that are painted with the fine wet hair of a brush, the artist's hand working up and down, across the large canvas. Hundreds of lines and each of them perfect—or almost perfect. The edge of the brush occasionally shows itself beyond the line it has formed. I begin to see the mind of Agnes Martin, the heft of years she spent in the desert.

Although this is art stripped of ego, it dawns on me I can see more artistic passion in this painting than anything else I have gawked at. The reclusiveness—what I considered eccentricity—is an armour worn to enable her to peel her skin away. Suddenly Rodin is as vulgar as Dalí. The opinion shocks me. It makes me uncertain of all my opinions. As I stare the grid seems to fade, so too the cream texture: I am staring into myself. Art, Pound says, is fundamental accuracy of statement. Truth was found with passion and commitment. The blood runs through my veins and the hair breathes on my skin. She says religion plays no part in her life. I look at Holfy, taking in what she is saying as if she is an apparition. It is as if her voice has been in my head and her presence—my *own* presence—startles me.

We scour New York together: the Met, the Guggenheim, the Frick, the Morgan. We are in the downtown Guggenheim again, looking at the Agnes Martin paintings. They still make no real sense to me—the blankness. *A depth and commitment to statement. She spent years in the desert.*

—She's full of herself. All ego.

Holfy looks at me and nods, not agreeing with me. Pride stops me from admitting I'm seeing it, seeing what she sees. All else is nonsense and a cheap trick. Truth had to be found with passion and commitment. This was what one did. What was true to the spirit.

—She's all ego and she doesn't believe in religion and she was years in the desert.

—Christ. It's worse than school with you.

She looks offended.

—I've been listening to you. I just don't see it. Let's go to Fanelli's.

We eat and talk about photographs. She talks about Fanelli's. She talks about her next project—photographing boxers. The food is good and she cheers up.

—Photography and boxing are immediate acts. With photography it depends on the way the camera is used. Photography can have an attitude that painting never can. Paint insulates the viewer.

I am tired listening to her. She's going on about Beaton and his snapshots—as she calls them.

—He's morally dishonest. He says he's getting behind glamour. Sure he is.

I am doubting her ethos. I think of her waiting for that moment when one's guard is down and she clicks and captures an ugly corner of the soul. Where is honesty? I have no idea what honesty or truth is. And I see I don't *know* Holfy any more than I

know why Agnes Martin trailed lines across canvas. Holfy lives
in the grove of uncertainty. That is her fascination.

Photography and boxing: two of her passions, two violent
acts. Sixty-five percent of New Yorkers, if asked, would refuse to
have their photograph taken, I read somewhere. We go back to
Beaton and agree we dislike the photographs for the same reason. He insisted he didn't take fashion shots. His work was
beyond fashion. It was art. Morally dishonest shit. The same is
true of Inge Morath. She, apparently, searched for the intelligence in her subjects as if this somehow portrayed a profound
understanding of humanity. Knickers.

Holfy rings and tells me her cat is not eating. When I come over
the cat is asleep, its purr deep as a drunken snore. We take the
subway to the clinic on the East Side. The veterinarian holds
Kahlo loosely in her coal-black hands and looks her over.

—She's not too good, is she?

—I know that—that's why I'm here.

The veterinarian looks over the rim of her spectacles and takes
Holfy in:

—Uh-huh. We can take tests. But she's very sick. You can get
some food down her with a syringe but—

—But what?

—She's very sick. She's suffering.

—She's told you that? My cat told you she's suffering?

The veterinarian purses her lips, looks at me, straightens her
spectacles and looks back to Holfy.

—That's my opinion.

We leave her in for overnight tests.

Holfy phones the clinic the next day. Kahlo has cancer of the throat. We take the subway over again with Kahlo's carrier box.

The same veterinarian sees us, her pink surgical gown splattered with dried blood:

—What do you want to do?

Holfy waves it all away from herself and walks out.

I wait while the cat gets the injection. She goes slack, her tongue peeping out her mouth playfully.

We take shelter from the rainstorm in the Bloomingdale's foyer. Cars and cabs scream at one another in the traffic jam. We step in from the street noise, dripping and steaming with rain. We dry ourselves as best we can.

—Who put her down?

—The nigger.

—Jesus. Don't say that word.

—The nice vet with the hip orange spectacles wearing the pink gown. Sorry about the N word. Doing what you do, pushing it.

—And you were there?

—Sure was.

She looks at the empty cat carrier in my hand and smiles painfully. When she recovers herself we set off through the labyrinth of perfumes and clothes. She stops an assistant and asks him about the density of a certain fabric. When she looks doubtful, he raises himself fully erect and mentions its durability. They discuss *resistance* and *fall* and *contour*, defining themselves through the way cloth is cut. Holfy presses a jacket against me and tells me to try it on. The assistant crosses some ill-defined social precipice and looks at me with tragic encouragement. He snaps the jacket in the air and holds it open:

—Adolfo Dominguez.

—Pleased to meet you.

He knows the jacket looks silly on me.

—Hey it's nice.

—It certainly is. It balances discipline with vitality. It gives him a rather potent air.

I'm on the verge of telling them both to go and shite but I think of Kahlo's body soft with death. I slip the jacket on. It has a price tag of $1,125. I feel like a tramp. My trousers are creased and my shoes need a polish. The store is too hot. Holfy tilts her head and tells me to pirouette.

—It does make a statement, says the assistant, picking at his moustache. With his crisp black suit and neat bow tie he looks like he could be on his way to a wedding if he took the measuring tape off from around his neck. Christmas carols dream of a white Christmas on the in-store music and make me dizzy.

—No, says Holfy finally as if disappointed in some failure of the Bloomingdale's jacket. The assistant leans on his aesthetic temperament, holds the ends of his measuring tape like extravagant lapels and sighs approval at her. Taking the jacket off I see the label is Dominguez and blush.

—I do need lingerie.

—One floor up, he says without blinking.

Holfy looks at me.

—Want to look around here awhile? We can meet up later.

We agree on the diner and she wipes the last streaks of tears from her face. All the stores are too expensive. But I do buy her something. I get her a soft puppet. It's a sheep, Lambchops. I open it and slip my hand inside it and go in search of her.

She is immersed in conversation with the store assistant, a tall elegant woman. They both throw back their heads in laughter. She buys a two-piece. On the way out, she stops and peruses some silver lingerie.

—Open the cat cage.

She drops several sets into the carrier.

—You're stealing?

—Be a detective when you grow up. Stolen lingerie turns me on.

—It's tagged.

She pulls me close with that waggling middle finger and whispers:

—Follow me.

We go through the Lexington Avenue exit and the alarm goes off. Holfy is already halfway down the subway steps.

—Let us go, you and I, and drink some cappuccino.

We face each other in the full subway, the cat carrier jammed between us.

—Will you eat with me tonight? I don't want to be in the apartment without her. Gerry is sick of you anyway.

Stuffed into the swaying subway with the smell of rain off our clothes, I see her as she must have been as a child sitting on the stairs.

—I'd be very happy to eat with you tonight. Let's get some food.

—There's stuff in the fridge.

—But it's not from Zabar's, is it?

—No. It is not from Zabar's.

—Well, let's do it then. We'll get a cab over.

—A cab—you in a cab?

—I get cabs. Sometimes.

The express rattles through station after station, each one a

blur of tiles and people. Our eyes avoid each other all the way
downtown. From there we get the taxi over to the store and then
over to the meat district.

I am here in the apartment in Gansevoort Street, here in my
future. I look around its vastness with the same hidden awe I feel
in the museums. A dog yelps somewhere and Holfy climbs over
her bed and up the steps to a window. A small black and white
creature leaps through from outside and lands panting on the
floor, nails scurrying on the rough wooden planks.

—What's that?

—*That* is Botero, the love of my life.

—But what is he?

—His breed you mean? He is a full-blooded American Boston
terrier. Take a shower.

—I'm fine.

—You smell of rain. I'd hate you to get pneumonia for being a
good boy scout.

—I'm fine.

—Irish Catholic, yes? Hah!

—Did anyone ever tell you that you can't pronounce pneumonia?

—As a matter of fact, yes. A little boy who can't pronounce his
th's told me. *Tanks for dese avocados and dose pears.* Well, Irishman, I'm
washing the filthy Eastside off me. Amuse yourself.

The sound of jazz from the bathroom. Gentle sound of running
water. Flatulent gurgles from pipes. Rush of piss gushing unapolo-
getically into the toilet. Her apartment is a cavern of delights.
Open shelving everywhere. I wander down to the living room.
Bookshelves reaching up to a sagging ceiling. A wooden steplad-

der to reach the top has become itself, a temporary bookshelf. The books have the look of having been explored years ago, exhausted. Around the corner is her studio. A desk dense with work. An entire wall is a corkboard for photographs, pinned with careful random-ness. Dozens of head shots; faces that exist only in New York. A yard-long panoramic shot of the AIDS flag being carried up Fifth Avenue. A series of nudes; shots of men's shoulders; legs; bends of elbows; hands in midgesture; backs. Landscapes of suffer-ing. Each shot is taut with grief. A photograph in the corner of the corkboard—a shot that doesn't fit the others, isolated from the clutter—a close-up of a woman's hand weary with age spots; hairless. The hand rests on the arm of a chair, a cigarette lazy between the fingertips. And beside the hand, a remote control. The shot is motionless except for a trail of indifferent ciga-rette smoke. It is the only photograph on the board with a title: *Mother.*

—Just because there are no doors does not mean it's yours to explore.

I turn around guiltily but she's not standing behind me. I look up, foolishly, half expecting her to be crouched on a shelf near the ceiling. No sign of her anywhere.

—Holfy?

—In the bathroom.

I don't know how I missed her—I see her now through stacks of folded towels. She has had shelving installed in what was once a doorway from the studio to the bathroom. This side of the shelving is walled with glass. She is brushing her hair over the toilet. Pulling tangles out. She must know I'm watching her. She puts a foot on the toilet and is drying her toes. I steal a last glimpse of her and turn back to the photographs.

❧ ❧ ❧

I am a parade of blunders. Walking around her apartment I should have known it: we were choosing each other. Thirty years of Holfy's art books. Margins full of tightly scribbled comments. On a book of photographs by Inge Morath, she has pencilled: *How can anyone be presented with so much and produce so little?* Hundreds of art books. Stieglitz, André Kertész, Ernst Haas, Fulvio Roiter, Juan Gyenes Remenyi, Ouka Lele, Lee Friedlander, Chagall, Franz Marc, Balthus, Agnes Martin, John Sloan, Magritte, Robert Tansey, Max Ernst, František Kupka, Mondrian, Picasso, O'Keeffe, Modigliani. Hundreds of art books. Biographies of painters and photographers. No novels.

—You've no Dalí, I shout back.

—Dalí was only for himself. He's irrelevant.

—And Picasso isn't?

—*Guernica?*

The toilet flushes. Guernica? Don't know what she means by that and ignorance of what my response should be silences me, pushes me on to another question.

—And no Monet?

—Simply a matter of taste. I don't like him.

—And no novels?

—The other wall. Around the corner for lit-rat-chure.

Some of her paintings are scattered on the walls—paintings and photographs mixed randomly. A glowing red painting with flecks of black and white. A noisy painting, impossible to locate the source of its sound. *Gansevoort Street.* It looks like something she might have done but it's not her signature: de Kooning. I lift it off its hook. It *is* a de Kooning. I almost drop it with fright. A separate bookcase; Kant, Camus, Sartre, Bertrand Russell, Plato, Foucault, Chrysippus, Pythagoras, Spike Milligan, Heidegger, Wittgenstein, Hegel.

She places a tray of tea things behind me. When I turn she is closer to me than I expect. A chartreuse turban tightly wrapped around her head, the effect making her eyebrows stark, her face stunning.

—Heard of any of them?

—You didn't give me the impression you were a reader.

—I forgive you, you're a man—you make mistakes.

—Wittgenstein lived in Dublin for a while. Used to go to the greenhouse in the Botanical Gardens to work in the winter because his room was too cold. Before I have time to finish the story she kisses me deftly on the lips.

—Don't get any ideas. They needed to be kissed, is all.

We sit on the sofa drinking a mixture of Assam and Earl Grey tea. She talks about going to Cooper Union in the early sixties. About trying to paint. About fucking as a political statement. She says the word *fucking* with such ease that it is difficult for me not to show surprise. I feel small in her presence. I know she is not trying to impress me and knowing this, she impresses me all the more. Her gruffness adds to her charm. This is an old self she is talking about, one she has discarded, one I hunger to inhabit, dead and all as it is. She tells me about Mazo and his infamous techniques: *Never mark a canvas unless you mean it.* She was too naïve to question him.

—He was respected in New York, still is, she says, smiling emptily. Making digital videos now. Made that famous one about the crazy Truman woman and her daughter. It had taken her twenty years to get past that perfection Mazo preached; hence the photography. All the time she is talking, I am wondering what her purpose is; there must be some purpose to her telling me all this. I pour more tea to appear at ease. It comes out thick and cold. I point to the kitchen and she nods. She continues talking, more loudly, while I potter about trying to find things. I interrupt her to ask her where she keeps the sugar.

—In the blue jug. O'Keeffe was in her eighties by then and New York was bestowing some or other award on her. I was covering the event for *People* magazine. They wanted *artistic* shots for the issue and somehow they got hold of my name. I took stills of paintings back then. I didn't do this kind of thing but I needed the money. I borrowed a Hasselblad from Roger (she points a finger to the large shot of the Woolworth building peaking through dense clouds) and did the job. My first celebrity shoot. O'Keeffe talked to me. I think because I was a female photographer. I changed direction with her. Are you listening?

—No.

Moving about her kitchen, searching for the tea strain, I am courting her.

—There is less responsibility in photography. At least I thought that until I met O'Keeffe.

I pour the tea. Holfy has beautiful hands.

—I discovered my cunt at the same time I discovered art. Art is about touching. Constantly touching. We have to create ourselves as art. You know, you always know a bad portrait photographer if he tells you to be yourself. There *is* no self. A photographer creates the self. She studies me bending with the tray. When I look up from the table it's as if she is looking for something in me, testing me. She is looking for listening, I think, if she is looking for anything; that's what people always want. The doorbell rings, a shrill, demanding noise. She ignores it and goes on.

—It has taken me a long time to know. I want nearness from a man. Art is about always touching canvas without meaning— without conscious meaning that is. Meaning is a foregone conclusion. That is what O'Keeffe did. I learned that over twenty years ago. I'm only beginning to be able to do it now. But that's not too bad. De Kooning only began to understand in the eighties and he's been after it all his life. You know the glaring mistake with all that shit (she waves towards the philosophy)? It's all written by men. How can we invent ourselves out of a male-only philosophy? I'm not talking about women. I'm talking about people. One should always fuck like the animals in the fields, don't you think.

De Kooning. The resolute way she said his name.

—You should take a cab. The subway is dangerous after midnight.

—I want you.

—That's nice. What for?

We stare at each other.

—You smell of marriage. Not attractive. Give it time. Maybe. You can sleep on the downstairs futon.

—I'll go.

—It's one in the morning.

—I'll go.

—You're not a sulker, are you?

—The worst. Hold grudges too. Forever.

I take the subway out of illogical spite. A black man, dressed like a dishevelled magician, does tricks with doves. The birds flutter up and down the train carriage. As the train grinds to a halt at Forty-second he whistles and the birds fly back to him and into their black box. I get off at Ninety-sixth to catch the local. Workmen are painting the station poles. The heat is stifling.

We don't see each other for a week. I break and call. She talks about New York and art and photography and her dead husband and her mother screaming at her father on long-distance phone calls. I can't imagine Holfy as a seven-year-old. I can't imagine her as a person other than the woman she is in front of me, the woman I have already created in my mind. I am terrified of her and know I will betray Ursula again and I haven't even touched Holfy. I haven't left Ursula. There would be no feeling of betrayal if I had really left her.

She is going to Pennsylvania to visit friends—partly because she can't bear the silence since Kahlo died. I offer to take care of Botero while she is away but she is taking the dog too.

—He doesn't miss Kahlo at all, treacherous bastard. If you want to be useful you could water the plants and collect the mail?

She spends hours packing and I sense, in her careful move-ments, she is already with them. I hate these people who make her whistle happily. I want to crawl inside her life. I want to pos-sess her. To know her more fully than she knows herself; to watch her dress in the morning. She takes an age to face the day and I want to see her create herself. I want to watch her buying her hats; watch her ask a shop assistant for this scent and that one; her ease at not feeling the need to make a purchase.

She takes me around the apartment and explains how much each plant needs. As she talks my life comes into focus. I remember when, as children, my cousin Brian and I were pillow fighting. I was getting the upper hand and in a fit of rage Brian threw down his lumpy pillow and leaped on me, screaming. He was stockier and stronger. I remember my eyes closing in pain as he clenched his fleshy fingers about my throat, his thumbs pressing on the Adam's apple. I knew Brian would strangle me he was so angry. It was my first realisation that my life could end and in one heave I tossed him over my head and his foot crashed through the bedroom window. I stood rubbing my neck, triumphant and terrified and relieved; such is my relief listening to Holfy. She is explaining about the outdoor plants. I see the years ahead with Ursula; can see what would happen with our lives; can see all the fights over her wanting to have a child, or worse, the silence over it, and I don't want to be responsible for any of it. I love her and can't live with such suffocating compromises. Holfy is still talking—something about Béla Bartók and flowers—and she catches sight of my mind drifting. I apologise. The fullness of life floods into me. How can I tell this woman, who hardly knows me, whom I hardly know, that I am planning to spend the rest of my life with her. She makes up the futon in the corner of the apartment that overlooks Gansevoort Street. You can sleep in my bed if you find it too noisy, she says. I shake my head that it will be fine right here.

Her phone rings constantly while she is away. She has told me not to answer it. Waking up feels like a sudden transportation into a deserted movie set. Each morning the meat trucks wake me before five. I stare out the window watching the men unload the meat. Then I go and shower.

I go through her books, one by one, fanning the pages, dust taking flight. I wipe down the bookcases and reshelve them, wondering which ones belong to her and which ones belonged—still belong—to Robert. His handwriting in the margins of many of them, little ticks by passages that pleased him. I look for naïveté in his comments, an emptiness in his intellect; find none. We have similar taste and it makes me dislike the ghost of his presence even more.

She has no vacuum cleaner. I find a broom and sweep out the apartment. I try to clean the windows with Windex but the grime is too thick. I wash them inside and out with hot soapy water, make tea while they are drying, polish the windows with the radio on the station she listens to, voices that become the voice of New York, more New York than the streets themselves.

The second night I lie in her bed, smell her off the sheets, imagine her sleeping in it with Robert, the conversations they had, the lovemaking. I pick up the book by her nightstand. *Public Opinion* by Walter Lippmann. I open it on the bookmarked page: I confess that in America I saw more than America; I sought the image of democracy itself. Alexis de Tocqueville. I read the chapter headings. What mind writes such a book? What mind reads it? Would Robert and Holfy have debated over it? I don't understand why I am so happy here.

When she returns she asks me if the noise disturbed me and I say yes and tell her she should move immediately. I like the meat

district. I grew up with screaming, she says. She smiles at the
tidiness of the place, asks if I am trying to ingratiate myself. Yes,
I say. Her directness is contagious. We agree on six hundred dollars a month, to be reviewed each month by both parties. Window cleaning welcome. Book tidying not.

She drives a blue Saab, and this evening we are driving uptown
to visit Barbara's bar, which is not doing so well. This is the
evening I realise we have been avoiding the obvious. I have
known her a year, been living here six months. We have never
touched except to jab each other playfully. She is asking me
about the painting job at Bradley's. Janis Joplin is singing on the
car radio. The bar is almost empty when we arrive. Holfy refuses
the free drinks. Barbara smiles at me, and her smile is that of a
professional politician, a smile that seems to say she knows
something about me, something I'm not even aware of myself. In
that moment, it strikes me how it looks as if we are a couple.

That night, I go to her bed. She smiles at me and shakes her
head. Slink back, she says. I ignore her finger pointing me back
to my corner. She sits up and glares at me and I retreat. I sleep on
my stomach, on the pain of hard desire.

Holfy's roof is full of large potted flowers, their clay containers
cracked and crumbling, life held together with wire and hope.
She spends hours here, watering the plants, pruning them, having dinner. Breakfast on a weekend morning on this roof is
heaven. She has a coq for cleanly lifting the head off a boiled
egg. She has an egg spoon with a serrated edge, perfect for

scraping the last morsel out of the thin base of the egg. She has spoons with deeper serrated edges for eating grapefruit. She has glasses that could never be filled with anything but orange juice. Small oval plates to accompany the boiled eggs. Napkins that cover the lap like small, heavy tablecloths.

The roof leaks badly that first summer and Gottleib blames Holfy and the weight of her plants. He threatens to remove everything. We rescue what we can before the roof is refelted. When the work is done she moves her plants back out, despite the warnings of the man who reputedly owns half of the meat district. The next day, when she comes home from work and climbs over the bed to the window she is confronted with a wrought-iron gate the size of a wardrobe, bolted onto the out-side wall. Her first reaction is to fight but I suggest another approach. We can call the fire department. The window is the only escape from the building other than the door. But she can't wait. She asks me to climb up on the roof and remove the gate. I climb up and fidget with the bolts. There are twelve. Some of the nuts are too tight, I lie. The pointing on the bricks looks fragile as if the mortar is crumbling like everything else on the street. I want to wait for the fire department. She asks me to try harder. I start to sing: tryyyy . . . tryyy . . . try just a little bit harder so I can lovelovelove . . . I kneel down, and tar, still wet in the summer heat, oozes from underneath the felt and sticks to my trousers.

—I don't care how long it's gonna take . . . Let's wait, please.

She nods. Moments later she is beside me on the roof and with one enraged yank she rips the cage off the wall. Fuck him, she pants, wiping her hands on her hips. The twelve bolts lie on the roof like spent cartridges.

That evening we drive across the village to Barbara's house

for dinner. Holfy has a way of pouring wine that enhances its enjoyment before it touches the lips. The glass should always be half full. A full glass of wine is aesthetically vulgar to the eye. I study her hands. They are brown with the fading summer. She is wearing the lapis ring that she and Robert bought years ago in Italy. Although her fingernails are bitten they do not have a pained look about them. Hers are delicate hands. Femininity and femaleness meet in these hands. Beauty is stored here.

As time wears on I begin to question everything, including Holfy. Ah, when the pupil turns the gaze on the teacher. I am painting apartments and working in a catering firm. At night, if I'm free, I assist Holfy at the weddings she is covering. We are both at home at the same time, and it makes it hard to breathe. I suggest making a room in the apartment, a space in a corner that would have room enough for a small desk. But Holfy refuses to build walls. She wants twelve hundred square feet of light. It would ruin the light and nothing mattered more to her in the apartment than light.

I am uneasy working illegally in New York. We should marry, she says, simply to deal with the problem. I am tempted but in my gut know that it is not the answer. It will only compound the problems. I am drowning, drowning in my infatuation with her, frightened of how well we click, and beginning to see how lost and rudderless I am, how much I miss the tedious familiarity of Ursula.

—Darling?

Holfy is looking at me over her spectacle rims. She looks her age tonight. She smiles and it is a smile filled with such affection that I feel sad. I want to tell her I love her but know, even

as the words form, that saying them is a selfish act: a pathetic
need to reassure myself. She puts her book down and holds her
arms out. I stare across at the Judd's Gym sign flashing in the
night.

—I'm farting tonight. Just to let you know the vastness of your
love must breathe in the foulest odour.

I laugh and pick up her book. Holfy is reading Rousseau. *Man
was born free, and everywhere he is in chains.*

—After Cooper Union. Never put a line on paper unless you
mean it, he said. I froze. I never put a line on paper. So I went to
ICP instead. Full of Europeans. *Photography is light,* the guy there
said. I'm from Iceland—there's nothing he could teach me about
light. As soon as I held a camera I knew. This was it. I felt the
relationship. The rest was struggling with being artistic. I knew it
was nothing to do with art. It was attitude. And Stillness. Light. I
didn't need to be told it was light, light was obvious. If you need
to be told that it is already too late. But I was shy then. I said
nothing. I made a mistake. For ten, fifteen years, I made a mistake. I hid behind the camera. Dead years. I won all the compe-
titions in the those dead years. An explosion of hate—which was
good to release but I didn't channel it. I directed it at the viewer.
I thought I was honest. So did all those judges. Olafsdottir is
unflinchingly honest. We were all wrong. I should have been
making it the essence of the photograph. Essence. Oops—*essence.*
Time to stop talking.

—An explosion of hate?

—For my dear parents. Who else can we hate with such devo-
tion?

The fragile and ancient hurt that seeps out of adults when they speak of wronged childhoods.

—I was raised by my mother after they divorced. My father got my brothers. My mother and I went to New York. She wasn't going to stay in Iceland, and Hungary was out of the question— even if she liked her in-laws. She sold the Icelandic International Travel Agency and we left. I was happy. That smelly room had been responsible for the first time my mother hit me—I asked her why we put International in front of everything. It's like living in a desert with a bodyguard, I said. Holfy lashes a hand through the air.

—She hit me a lot after that.

—And your father?

—My father. My father is my father. What else to say? I got to admire him a lot—when I had to live alone with my mother. When we all lived together I thought all the arguments were his fault. I thought the divorce was our fault, my brothers and I. Then I thought it was my fault. Years later, I looked at my mother and saw, as they say in America, she was the key player. My therapist— imagine a little village girl from Iceland having a therapist—asked me what is the one thing that sticks with me about my mother. *Are you listening.* The therapist said yes, and I said no, that was what I remember. Are you listening. I did nothing but listen to my mother.

—Her husband.

—Robert was with Lavansky. The aeronautics Lavansky—not the painter. That's what brought us together. Painting. He called

me his chiaroscurist. I thought he was ribbing me when he said
he tested helicopters. You mean whether they crash or not? I
asked him and he nodded. Do they? I asked. Sometimes, he said.
And he was so genuinely nonchalant that I fell for him there and
then. Holfy's face takes on a softness. She loves his memory too
much for me ever to grow fond of him. I pour her some fresh coffee, go into the kitchen to wash the dishes. She continues talking
through my drying.

—He crashed five times, you know that? Five times and never
a scratch.

—What about the sixth?

It's out before I can help myself.

—You're a *cruel*, blue-eyed angel.

—Sorry.

—He was coming home. Midweek. He had been up at Lavansky's. He was a real man. She blows me a kiss, takes off the purple chinese jacket. Underneath, a pale pink man's shirt. She
waves her hands in front of her reddened face.

—Hot flushes. That stage of life. He was coming in through
the Queens tunnel. I never understood that. He always came in
on 1. Always. And down the Hudson Parkway. He liked to get a
look at the Palisades. He used to say *Imagine what it was like when
they first came in and saw the Palisades. New York must have been something
else then.* He liked the snatches he could glimpse of the Empire.
He and it were born the same year. It's why he liked my place so
much—he'd stand at the window and say *Our precious inch of
Empire.* He never ceased to be enchanted with New York. A car
broke down in the tunnel in front of him. And then, in the other
lane, going in the opposite direction, the same thing happened

in almost the exact same spot. One in each lane at the same time. They had to reverse in trucks at either end. Traffic backed up in both lanes. When they towed out the car in front of Robert, he didn't move. He was dead. He had had a heart attack. She laughs at the absurdity.

—A man who risks his life in the sky and dies underground. You have to have a sense of humour, yes?

I stare out the window at the mauve inch of the Empire State. Precious inch. The city seems full of love. The time I went to the top with Ursula when we visited New York. She sneaked up behind me as I leaned against the rail and slipped her arms through mine and brushed her fingers over my chest. Such bliss it was; the view of Manhattan and her. Hot dogs and sticking stamps on postcards and running my hand over her arms. The silence at the top; no horns, no sirens, no whoosh of hot subway train, no screaming miseries; nothing but breeze and dampness of clouds. I was still translating dollars and punts in my head, a tourist. Such a long time ago it seems. My eye catches sight of an ant traipsing up the windowpane; it pauses on the Empire's tip, peaking over the Village, over all of us. His minuscule legs leading him nowhere. He crawls with vital importance to the top of the glass; reaches the edge; stops; hurries with magnificent urgency to the bottom. He marches up again, and halfway, turns and scurries daintily to the left. Three is such randomness in his movements and he makes decisions with such haste that it's impossible to imagine there is a rationale behind his decision to turn left and not right. And yet there must be. I consider crushing him with the back of my thumbnail to end his frustration but stop myself: God must watch the world with the same indifference.

Ursula. Longing for her overcomes me. The scent of her skin,
seeing her laughing in the bed as we read those dreadful review
books together.

I wash and dry the last glass. Holfy is sitting with her coffee,
scraping at the wax that had spilled from the candleholders onto
the wooden table. I sit down again and look at her. We look
fixedly at each other for a long time. Then I stand up, the chair
screeching on the tiled floor. I stoop and kiss her. She stands and
kisses me back. Her mouth tastes wonderful. Even barefoot she is
taller than I am. I pull away from her. I pick up the Eliot poems
I've been reading and go into the darkroom. She potters around
for a while, talks on the telephone.

—What you doing?
    —Reading. Bed.
    She frowns and shakes her head.
    —Ms. Olafsdottir. I didn't want to presume.
    —Excellent pronunciation. Can you fuck too?
    She nods her head for me to follow her.

She hands me a towel and tells me to shower. She tells me to
hurry. A large curling turd floats in the toilet. Her own sweet
smile. When I come out she tells me I am not supposed to get
dressed again. Undress, she says. She sits by the fireplace and
watches me. She tells me to lie down and to touch myself. I lick

a finger and caress the tip of my nose. She tells me I must be serious. She takes straps from her travel case and ties my wrists to
the bedposts. I am nervous, excited, fight a smile. She kisses my
lips, my chest, my cock. She kisses my toes. She ties my ankles
to the bedposts.

—Where did you get the ropes?

—My yoga ropes.

—Yoga ropes.

—Stop talking.

She unbuttons her shirt and looks at me looking at her purple
bra. She grins and looks down at herself, grabs her own breasts.
Then she pulls on a pair of yellow leather gloves. She lifts her
skirt to her hips and gets on top of me. My stomach tenses under
her wetness. She slaps me gently. I start to laugh unable to take it
seriously. She shakes her head in warning. She holds my cock
with her gloved hand, finds her opening, and encloses me. She
rises up and down, slaps me hard. My face burns through my
smile.

—Tell me when to stop.

She slaps me harder.

—Tell me when.

I look at her, at the world she is entering. She hits me again.
My eye closes in pain. Her wetness running down my stomach,
turning cold. She hits with both hands now as if swatting flies.
The pain seeps into the back of my closed eyes. I am listening to
her breathing, to her squelching pleasure. She is holding my ears
and kissing my mouth, kissing my mouth and licking my lips, my
nose, my eyelids. She licks my ears and says something. She
repeats words in what must be Icelandic. She punches me in the

face and any sense of the erotic vanishes. In English she tells me to open my mouth. She clears her throat, and spits into my mouth. She thrusts harder and harder until my pelvis bone hurts. She comes and comes, rubbing into me slowly until at last she spreads her heavy body on me and is calm. I am hard, unspent. But she is lost in herself and my excitement wanes. Powerlessness has its own passion, its own relief.

We sleep through the day and fuck and eat and sleep and fuck. Someone rings the doorbell persistently in the early afternoon but goes away. We hear car doors slam throughout the day, laughter from the lunch tables outside Florent. We settle into our own silence. I want to ask her why yellow gloves? If the game goes both ways, if I should hurt her? She is lying on her stomach, reading. I rub her back, move down to her buttocks. She spreads. I wet a finger in my mouth and find her anus. Violation, more than anything, arouses Holfy. I go in behind her. Lovelylove-lylovelylovely.

We are whispering to each other in the groggy morning. She is lying on top of me, beached. I ask her is there any advice she remembers her father gave her to carry through life.

—O, yes. *Say thank you.* My father works for the United States government. He is very polite. Very civilised. She looks at me to check if I am following. I amn't.

—He was on the Manhattan Project. Oppenheimer's favourite scientist—besides himself. The telephone rings. We lift our heads to see the time. It's after five in the morning. I think it might be my father calling. I always think an early call is him phoning to give bad news. She answers as if she's been awake hours. It's the first conscious realisation I have of disliking something in her: this need to always appear switched on.

—Hi Jay.

Kleinmeyer. An art dealer she had a brief affair with—he was buying some of her husband's paintings. I met him once at an art dealer's house on Claremont Avenue. She was so at ease there, drifting between the big money, pointing out Grant's Tomb across Riverside Drive. It was more an art gallery than a home. She's loquacious with him. She rolls away from the phone smelling of his power. How could she touch such a pig of a man. Belly vast against his designer shirt. It disgusts me that she let this fatso inside her body. She has told me she would do anything for a man who could do something unexpected. *You men are all so fucking predictable.*

—He must have had to come in behind you.

She looks at me, baffled, her phone smile fading.

—You know, with that belly of his in the way.

She grimaces. I get up and shower, soaping myself with the soap she uses. The plastic blow-up duck, Newt, nudging my legs. Her slender legs when she showers. One of her hairs on the soap.

I go to Florent for coffee. Reggie is serving. The face of Greta Garbo and the style of Madonna. I have never felt fully at ease with Reggie; I had an erection the first time I saw him dressed as Edith Piaf. Then I learned she was a he.

—Tiff?

He pours me a coffee and pushes the cup forward like a delicate floral arrangement.

—She's a motherfucker.

—Biscotti?

I nod. Reggie is wearing a silver silk bra with a matching silver miniskirt. His skin is flawless.

—I'd like to get her and—

—Now now, I'm easily shocked Mick. Do let me know when you discover your true orientation. I *adore* leprechauns.

He blows a kiss and totters off. A black is rooting through a Dumpster across the street. I am as sick of New York as much as I am sick of her. Her eagerness. All that shit about the sixties. Anything is possible. Anything. She comes in. Waves Reggie away. She sits down heavily beside me, pulls the coffee over by its saucer, twirls it, and sips.

—I don't sleep with him anymore. But I need the business. I have to be smooth with him. He gets off on it. He could give the Maxim's jobs to anyone.

—You do well enough.

—It's not a money thing. I want to make it with the photography. *Really* make it.

—And you need him?

—Him? Everyone.

She's so full of contradictions. I don't know where to start.

Andrew Raposa, indignant writer for *The Nation*, comes in and joins us. I beam at my escape, and stand up.

—Here, Andrew. I've been keeping it warm.

—You going so soon?

—No he's not. We're having a conversation here Andy, okay?

Andrew holds his hands up and walks backwards away from us. I smile awkwardly at him and he waves an understanding hand. She'll stay and talk with him about this, and I feel myself close a little more.

❧ ❧ ❧

She rolls over to my side. Her touch is an apology. I hate her. I turn and kiss her. I smile the smile she likes. We kiss. I caress her between her legs until she moans. I watch her pleasure.

—Turn over.

—Not yet.

Her eyes are closed.

—Turn over.

She gets up and turns. I go in fast and she takes in a breath, steadies herself. I plough as hard as I can into her. My anger bangs against her for all its worth. I am so angry I can't come. I grip the fat on the sides of her buttocks and keep going, digging my nails into her. The sweat rolls off me and I begin to lose my breath. I think of hitting her hard and that does it—I come—and I pull out of her and sit panting on the bed. She gets up and lights a cigarette.

—Hey, that's the first time we came together.

I wipe the sweat out of my eyes and give her the finger. No matter how bad it is with her, it is always intoxicating. Such pleasure in taking Holfy without ceremony. Once, just after she's gone to the toilet. No time to wipe herself. That is the sin. To go further than desire.

She gets Photoworld, Good Gardener, Roof Gardens, J. Crew, Caring, Victoria's Secret (not for the clothes, she says), Lands' End, L.L. Bean, Tweeds. A dozen catalogues, at least. As many magazines arrive for Robert Dead Husband. Alumni magazine from NYU, Daedalus Books catalogue, Film World, marketing blurb from Lincoln Center. The Time Machine Company catalogue. Palladium Numismatics. Pieces of his life.

A Mr. Kutzko telephones looking for RDH:

—He's not here. He's dead.

—I'm dreadfully sorry, says Mr. Kutzko.

—You sound it.

—Excuse me?

—You need to update your listings. He died three years ago.

—Is Mrs. Tansey available?

I hang up on his Armani voice. New York never stops selling. Even the *New York Observer* comes with his name on it. Robert is everywhere. I share Holfy with a dead man.

In summer she does her tai chi on the roof. She started it with Robert the week before he died. Occasionally I look up from the worktop and stare out the window and there she is: arms outstretched, knees bent, the light fabric of her culottes flapping. She has the grace of a swan. When she comes in, I wash the roof tar off her feet with a basin of warm water and rub peppermint lotion into her toes. Bronzed and papery her feet are with age. I rub tiger balm on the pain in her lower back. She is the centre of my happiness.

She drinks vodka gimlets. Any drink that requires a mixer is a good drink in her eyes. I ask her to make me a manhattan. You want to drink New York, she says, without looking up from her negatives. She sits in her Bloomingdale's underwear most evenings, when she wears underwear. She wears a black bra and no knickers and manages to look both dressed and coordinated. She understands the rippling secrets of fashion. I like the smell of her sweat, her juice, enjoy waiting for Holfy to do her face in the

evening. The transformations. Clothes reveal her mood. Surface
is everything, she says one night. We are on the roof garden at
the Met, watching the orange sun glide between buildings. Surface is everything. One of those irritating catchphrases that she
is so good at pluming in front of me. Indeed, I say, watching the
sun drop out of sight. She picks up my tone of voice and looks at
me like I am a stranger. The distance of years seeping between us.
I realise I don't know her at all. All the talk we share, all the
books, the music, is irrelevant in the face of this.

I go into the bathroom, look at myself in the mirror and feel far
from home. I sit down on the edge of the bath and stare at the
prints on the wall. Lichtenstein and Haring. I never really liked
them. I am being unfair to her. She had these a long time, before
they were known. There is other art crammed on the wall, most of
the artists unknown. I am looking for a reason to dislike her. As if
to taunt me I smell her cigarette smoke. She smokes Marlboro
when she can't get Gitanes, smokes with the kind of urbane
sophistication that makes me want to start smoking again. I am trying to insert myself into life as if it were some intricate board game.

She comes into the bathroom and stands in front of me. She
reaches down and scratches my head and I press the side of my
face to her warm stomach. We stroke each other. We kiss and she
sits on the edge of the sink. It is not making love. It is not fucking either. Afterwards I ask her what it is and she says she doesn't
know what it is but whatever it is it is not ineffable. She asks me
never to use the word ineffable and she asks me to stop looking
for truth. Approximate, she says.

❦   ❦   ❦

Days pass, and then weeks pass and we don't talk about the
future. Her friends say nothing. People are happy that we are
happy. And people—at least the people we know—don't really
want to know about my life in Ireland. This is New York City and
we live in the present and the edgy excitement of what we might
do next weekend is as far as we take ourselves. Approximate.
This is all we ever do. There are no facts. Buildings are facts.
Trees are facts. But trees and buildings fall and disappear as
quickly as love between people disappears.

I am tying Holfy by the wrists and feet to the window gate with
the yoga straps. I stand there looking at her moist haunches. The
basin between her feet. She is wearing the silver shoes. The skin
slack on the underside of her buttocks. Memories chink in my
head like glass bottles. Ursula looking at me in disgust. I look at
the contraption in my hands and I can't do it. The pause tells her.

—Don't worry about it. It's who you are. Who I am. You've
discovered a boundary in your life. Hooray. Untie me you
scoundrel and let's go do a New York thing.

It doesn't deflate the humiliation. I lovehate her for making little of the failure. We go and do the NYT as she calls it and eat
Merluza a La Vasca at Café San Martin. We have a bottle of
Albarîno. She has strawberries and cream. I eat the natillas. She
plucks the ends off the strawberries and flicks them into the ashtray.

—You see, there's the hull and here's the strawberry disappear-
ing into my greedy mouth.

—Fuck off.

—O, dear, *who knew?*

She reminds me about the day in Central Park when we hired a boat and fucked on the secluded rock. Then she rowed off and abandoned me. We laugh at the memory but the evening is gone from us. Another wall discovered. Another loss. Leaves suddenly falling.

The message stuck on the kitchen table: *Your father is sick. Go home. Take a taxi for once in your life. Flight at 7. Seats available. If you're home by 4 you might make it to airport. Sorry. I'll wait. Will always wait.*

Botero jumps on hind legs looking for biscuits. I call Muriel but there's no answer. Then Aidan but no answer there either. I scribble on Holfy's note that I'm going and will call her from the airport. I pick up one of her cameras. I regret not having a photograph of Ruth in her last days. Might as well get one of him. He better be dying.

There's a long queue to the metal detector. A woman is pleading with security about her pram.

—The pram has to go through.

—But they're asleep.

—You'll have to take them out. The pram goes through, ma'am.

It's fun to fly; to watch other people's distress.

There is a phone in the seat of the airplane. I pull it out and look at it but it needs a credit card to operate. Fumbling, I try to get it back in the slot. The man next to me taps me and asks if I want to use it, if it's a short call. Three words. My credit card can spring for three words, he says. *I'll wait, too,* I say to her answering machine. Wonder how much it costs to whisper three words into an answering machine flying over the Atlantic Ocean?

Father

The flight is a blank. I wait at the baggage carousel for fifteen
minutes before I remember I haven't brought any luggage.

I had forgotten rain. It is early morning yet the Dublin sky is
so dark it might be a winter afternoon. Mater Hospital, I say to
the taxi man with as little drama as I can manage. Ah, nothing
serious? says he. Hope so, says I, sitting back and staring out the
window. In the rearview mirror I see his mouth laughing the
laugh of the ignoramus. The city is miserable with the fat cries of
seagulls. I thought the familiarity would excite me. I had told
myself I loathed going back but it isn't true, I'm thrilled, thrilled
even by the chattering taxi man who pierces me with asinine
questions. I tell him I keep up with news. They have it all on

computer now, I say, in the hope of heading off the lecture. He
goes on and on, filling the car with a changed Dublin. *Too late for
me now it is, all this boom. I'm fiftyeight. It's fellahs your age will be making
it.* He manages to make me a stranger in my hometown. The
Dublin epidemic: to let the newly returned know they do not
know their city. I have always loved this city. People talk. They
are articulate and funny and hardy and hopeless at confronting
reality and I like them. As we draw nearer to the city centre,
depression pools about me. Familiar sights clamour, invading the
husk of myself. An advertisement for Smithwick's beer. My
throat is dry from travel. The greenness of Irish buses. An advertisement introducing a fast route from Dublin to New York. It
must be great over there, he says. Once, coming home from her
studio, I told Holfy that the best thing about New Jersey was the
view of Manhattan. Her laughter; her womanly laughter pos-
sesses me. I look at my watch. I could have breakfast in Bewley's,
get a taxi back to the airport, buy a ticket there and be in Greenwich Village by five. I could buy some cakes in that patisserie on
Bleecker Street. I imagine her driving through the Holland Tunnel with the windows rolled up tightly. I could be waiting for her
to push backwards through the door, arms laden with work. I
could be sitting there, waiting for her to set down her camera
equipment and lift her head with slow surprise when she hears
me humming. Trouble is, he says, the taxis over there is like
cages. You have to be fenced in.

In his hospital deathbed, Daddy tells me I was such a lovely little
boy. Full of zest, he says, smiling. He is smiling into the past at
the ten-year-old boy who idolised him. Who ran to get another

bucket of hot water. Who squeezed the water out of the dirty rag into the gutter. The boy who loved working. The boy who didn't want to go home at the end of a long summer day when other boys were enjoying the freedom of their holidays, my freedom being a man like Daddy.

—Like a young gazelle, he says.

—I was.

Full of immense fondness for his lost son. He smiles as if that boy will emerge out of the disappointment standing before him. Daddy, I want to say, I didn't want to go home after the day's work because I knew there'd be a fight. You'd pick a fight with Ruth. They took it in turns. I worked hard with you Daddy because I didn't want to go home to our screaming life. You never knew anything, Daddy. You are a stupid and selfish bastard and you don't deserve me at your side. I look into his bleary eyes and am moved to a lie.

—Those were the days.

—You're right, there. No truer word spoken. Zest. You were full of zest. Is Canning still annoying you?

—Not any more. I don't work at the spraying now. I'm in New York now.

—A kick in the chestnuts is the only answer for cornerboys like him. I grew up with his sort. They put a shirt and tie on and think they're different. Where did you say?

—In New York.

—Aren't you the big shot. You won't reck us now. You're your own man now with your own face.

I nod at him, wanting to get out but his eyes lock on me, he's not done, knows these last days are his.

—Don't remember do you, what you said after your mother left?

I should have left before the drugs, mixed with nostalgia, started working on him. I shake my head for him.

—One night you were crying in your bed and I came over to you and you asked me who would you look like now that she was gone. Everyone always said you were the spit out of her eye and you were worried you wouldn't look like anyone now that she was gone. And I told you you'd look like yourself and that every day you'd look more and more like yourself. You used to ask me, Do I look like me today? And I'd say you look very much like you. There's a lot you forget about yourself that your old Da remembers, don't forget that. We're not all gobshites just because we don't have the secondary school education. If you ever see her, your mother, tell her there's no hard feelings.

—None from you maybe. Maybe when I'm kicking the bucket I'll feel the same. Not now though.

I phone Ursula and listen to the beeps on her machine. Busy girl. I go for a drink, call her again, go back to the Mater, he is sleeping. In the morning he will tell me he hasn't slept a wink. I call her again. Still the machine, even more beeps. I walk down Eccles Street and stand at the corner thinking about what to do. Toetapping on the corner. What to do to do to do. Muriel has said I can stay with her. She made no mention of Ursula but the invitation says it all. I cross the road to get a bus into town. The 16 passes, going the other way. I recognise the driver from the years getting the bus out to Clastronix and wave. Only people I know anymore are strangers. I stare across at Birmingham's where we often went for a drink when we lived over Youkstetter's. She would meet me there after I came out from visiting Ruth. Should

call it The Waiting Room. Or The Morgue. Before and after. No
bus comes. Impulsively I wave down a taxi and ask him to go to
the house in Dalkey.

Her car isn't there. I think about going back into town and staying at Muriel's but then decide I'll wait. I pay the driver and walk
up the driveway. Willy is sitting there, watching me. She rises up
off the windowsill, stretches, and jumps pertly onto the gravel.
She's got big. Lost the kittenishness. She walks over and rubs
against me. No sign of Vomit. Out hunting. Vomit was always
the wild one. I sit on the bench in the front garden. No sound
anywhere. The cat jumps up on me. Darkness falls about the
house. The cat drifts off and after a while I hear the flap slap back
and forth. She's gone into the heat. A light goes on in the house
and startles me, making me feel like a thief. Through the high
window over the hall door I see her turning slowly on the stairs,
her back to me. I walk up the garden, and passing the garage,
realise the car must be in there. She would have cleared everything out by now. Bye-bye books. The overhead sensor picks up
my form and the outside light comes on. I knock on the door.
She pulls the curtain aside and looks out. A slow unlocking of
bolts.

—You got here fast.

I start to tell her to back off. The news of my father will deflate
trouble, at least for now. She turns and I see the bruises on her
face. She shifts and faces me. She is centuries older. The hall is
quivering with silence.

—What happened your face?

—Hi husband still.

She closes her eyes.

—I was attacked. Didn't Mum tell you?

—Attacked?

—On the hill. They got in the car. Come in. Welcome home.
Vomit runs in between our legs, meowing.

—Who did?

She closes her eyes again.

—The children. The hill on the corner where the car sometimes stalls. It cut out and as I was starting it one of them jumped
in beside me and shouted to the others to push it. I just started it
again and then the others got in the back. They made me drive
around. It was a blast. She goes ahead into the kitchen. I am
taken aback by its vastness. She has had all the downstairs walls
demolished. She lies on the sofa by the fire and pulls the blankets
up around her.

—Want some tea?

—Where did it happen?

—What do you mean where? The hill. Where the car cuts out.
It doesn't matter where. They did things to me.

She stops talking and lies back down. I lie down beside her
and hold her tightly, expecting a struggle. But there is no struggle. She is motionless on the sofa like a drunk. I see the card I
sent her from New York propped up over the fireplace. Two signs
like interstate directions over a highway: Men who comb their
hair to hide their bald spots. Women who put too much effort
into relationships.

—I bet they've burned out the car. Pigbastards. I'd love to roast
their smelly balls.

—What did they do?

I dread the answer.

—They felt me. They put their hands all over me as I was driving.

—Why didn't—

I stop myself. Lord save me from asking stupid questions.

—I'll live with the whys, thank you. There were two boys and Darina. One of the boys was Larry. I don't know who the other one was. I hate them. I hate her most of all. She put her hands between my legs. She spat in my hair. I drove them around for an hour. Jesus I was so stupid. I always lock the doors.

I can't believe she is telling me this. I can't believe the children from Irishtown followed her. What was it with them?

—Have you reported the car?

She looks at me with tired, cynical eyes, an older woman now.

—I told the police. It won't make any difference. Why won't they leave me the fuck alone?

—Where's your mother?

—At work. She'll be here soon, she says, looking up at the clock on the mantel. I told her not to phone you. There was no point in you coming home.

—She didn't. At least she didn't get me. My father is dying. I got the call yesterday. I didn't know about this.

—That makes me feel better—really. I didn't want you here because of this, because of them. Sorry about your Dad.

—I would have come.

—Easy on the sugar. Want to see around the place? Lot of changes.

—It looks wonderful. Never imagined it could not feel damp. You shouldn't get up.

—I'm fine. Just tired.

The stairwell is the only part of the house that is not done up, bare walls, the newel missing from the top of the staircase. We

go into the bedroom. *Her* bedroom. I am a guest who knows
where the hot-water bottle is kept, which drawer stores the cutlery. The photograph of the two of us taken on top of the Empire
State Building is gone. The colour scheme is the same as Bath
Avenue. She has held on to some of our choices—if she ever
thought they were ours. I tell her about Daddy, that he really is
dying.

—Where are you staying? I don't mean to sound rude.

—I'm staying with an aunt.

—The Muriel I met at Ruth's funeral. She's a character.

—Yup.

—You're quite the Yank.

—I used to accuse you of that.

We smile at the history between us.

She is asleep now, deep in the drowning nightmare. A jugger-
naut screeches to a halt outside, its brakes hissing and sighing.
She whimpers in her howling sea. I wait for the tension to leave
her body, ease onto the bed and rock her slowly in the nest of my
lap. She clings to safety. Her eyes open, full of shock and relief.
She stares into my face, still fighting the maw of waves. I speak
without thinking.

—I want it to work. I want us to be together.

She turns her head into the pillow. What to do with the bag of
feelings I have left for her? What to do with everything that's
gathered like dust in some forgotten room? All the intimacies
that made up our life.

My father dies happy with the inaccurate knowledge that I love
him unconditionally. There is no reason to forgive a life of pro-

found ignorance. The insignificant moment of his death is a lame reason to forgive sixty-two years of a life flooded with self-absorption. There is no resentment. I will not wound my life with bitterness. But I will not cajole myself, or be cajoled into some cathartic understanding of who he was and why he was the way he was. He was wrong too long. There is no resentment. There is no absolution. Would need to know all to forgive all. I know more than enough. How can one know a man who lived every spare moment in front of a television, believing in his heart that his wife might walk back in any moment and all would be well?

Back at Muriel's house I start to cry and people are relieved by my grief. I am not crying for him. I am crying for Budgie, the blue bird we had when I was five. We fed him too much and he used to sit on the bottom of his cage, incapacitated with fatness. His nails were curled like the swirls on a snail's shell. I'd hold Budgie's scared body in my hand and my father would clip his nails. We were in a hurry to get to Mass and he cut a nail too high up and Budgie bled and died. I never forgave him for being in a hurry out to Mass. I watched him pass the collection basket down through the congregation, smiling at everyone. My father had a smile for everyone. Except us. Daddy: everyone's handyman.

I am gardening in the front when her father comes with that woman he married after he divorced her mother. He asks if he can do anything. *If.* You can go fuck yourself.

—She's resting.

—We shouldn't disturb her then.

—Not at all. You've driven so far. She'd be upset if I didn't wake her.

He leans against the car, cornered. Even in the vulgar face of drama we are cripplingly polite to one another. Rachel is her name, the woman he married. Rachel. Chalk squealing on a blackboard. Everyone was so surprised, so *shocked* with his choice. I think her a perfect selection after Ursula's mother: a mannequin who spreads her legs for him. He walks around the garden looking at the roses, flattering this and that. His forte was always to stand in the garden and talk of greenfly and blackfly and aberrations. Now he babbles about how well we have done. He is of the brigade who gets too nice too late. He hoicks up the knees of his pants and squats to sniff the Peace rose. He looks up at me, vaguely guilty eye, like a dog caught in the middle of a shit. He stands abruptly and goes up to the house. He approaches it as if it is a sleeping tiger. Rachel asks me about the flowers. She is being a woman, engaging the man. Talk to him. Ask him questions. He will adore you for adoring him.

—Flowers are such an important part of us, she says.

—Fuck flowers.

She looks at me a long minute. I continue digging.

—I could fuck on them perhaps, on their petals. Hardly with them.

I stop digging, lean on the trowel.

—I'm sorry.

She shrugs. She is used to not existing. I can think of nothing to say that makes a difference. Sorry. A word to make me feel noble to myself. I lift the small tree out of the boot of the car and sit it on the gravel. It looks tremulous, nervous of its surroundings. I cut off the black plastic holding pot. Roots.

—They don't get on, do they, she says, looking back to the house.

—No. He doesn't like women, not even his daughter.

She smiles without feeling.

—Rachel, it's not a great time. I didn't mean you. I'm sure he—

—You should have been a priest. No, a bishop. The speaker of great truths.

I set the tree in the bed, push in hills of soil around its base. Go away. I want all of them to go away. Rachel standing there aware of the freshness of her beauty, of what it allows her; her breasts suggest she has solutions. Every time I meet her I try to like her and fail.

—Why did you marry him?

—For the sex. Why did you marry her? Surely not the money.

I look up at her answer and she pouts her disappointment. I had hoped the question would get rid of her but instead it satisfies her. She must be asked that question often.

—The truth is even more shocking. I married him so as not to be alone. Yippety doo dah.

I press the soil in firmly with the heel of my foot. Already, it is establishing itself, its tiny leaves finding a breeze. She refuses to go.

—An altruistic gesture?

—What?

She nods towards the tree.

—You're not going to be here to see it grow, are you?

—No.

She reaches out and touches my arm. I can't bear to think about any of this. She has mouthed words that no one else would dare. This is the one thing I do like about her. We go up to the house and put the kettle on. He must be still up there in her bedroom. The memory of her parents' divorce when she was six flashes into my mind. He had gone into her bedroom and pleaded with her to stay, to choose him. The air is damp. I wish I was in New York. Wish I was lying on Holfy's warm body. I make the tea; a truce. Rachel tells me about her life in Stillorgan. Of raising Ursula's brothers and sister. Her words blur in my mind; they become past tense, her life is decided, resolutely directed. As she talks (it's about how the children play on her not being their mother) I catch sight of a toy on the kitchen shelf. It's the little Latvian doll I bought for Ursula the day Holfy and I had lunch in McSorley's. We came out of the pub a little drunk, and it was raining and we took shelter in the doorway of the store. It's a little wooden russian doll. It sits beside the tea canister, untouched in its cellophane wrapper.

Our life ended with the completion of the house. The state of the marriage went in inverse proportion to the state of the house. If it were a graph, it would be a clean X. The strange patterning of life. Ursula explaining about Fibonacci numbers. He loves me, he loves me not. It will always be *he loves me*, she explains. Nature and numbers colluding. Only if the flower is complete, I say. Yes, she says, it depends on perfection. The smell of her cunt is as vivid as the smell of cut grass. I am a fool.

As I'm walking them both to the car he says that Ursula is in a bad way. He is impressed with his courage to say something as intimate as a feeling his daughter might be having. He manages to sound like a rather perplexed doctor. Rachel moves, on the verge of being the soothsayer. She stops herself. I resist the involuntary urge to nod, to agree with him in any way. He looks down, kicks the tyre of his Volvo.

—You'll work it out, so, he says.

His nose twitches at the air; gesture made; he's gone the extra mile; more than many a man. Vomit wanders up the driveway. When she reaches us she arches, looking for a reason to ignore us. Rachel stoops and pets her. Even in her stoop Rachel acts being a woman; she flattens the back of her skirt beneath her buttocks as she bends; flattens the front of it when she stands. Always a woman wanting to be wanted.

—Do you want to know?

—I beg your pardon?

—Do you want to know about Ursula and me? About working it out.

—You don't have to go into—it's not our business, the details of your—

—Because if you want to know I'll tell you. But if you don't want to know that's very good too. You can have it either way but you can't have it both ways.

Her father is exhausted. Even with the sun glinting off his heavy spectacles I can see the struggle to contain his anger. A woman passes by at the end of the drive looking at the house as if it's a dress she's considering buying. Gooooey, I yell, waving to her. She hurries on. The old man makes a decision. He's going to drop the pretence. He puts a hand on my shoulder.

—You do whatever you think is right in the eyes of God. Let's leave it at that.

He pats me on the shoulder and gets into the car. I am stunned, not by the aggressive hand on the shoulder (I am used to the patronising pats of other men) but by the mention of God. I expect God to appear and tell us all to go to hell. Rachel

extends her hand. I want to hurt her, to make sure the old bastard's day worsens:

—Good luck, whore.

—It's not about luck, sweetie.

She winks, seats herself with ladylike aplomb in the car, and
waves as she closes the door. I can tell he's asking her what was
said. Drive David, she says loudly. The core of us is aloneness.
Rachel is nearer than any of us. She knows herself and knows too
she can live with him without compromising what matters most
in her life. Strange, I never thought of Ursula's father having a
first name. I sit on the garden bench long after they've gone. He
was a child once, had a mother yelling *David* at teatime. A lawn
is being mowed somewhere, far enough away to sound nothing
more than a bee buzzing. The sun, exhausted, has given the last
of its heat to the day. Night comes. The bathroom light goes on.
Timid tinkling. The pull of the toilet chain and a clang. No flush.
Another pull, more violent. Nothing. I rise to go and help her
with it. The light goes out. I stop halfway across the lawn.
Already back in bed by now.

Separate, it's what we both want.

I walk down to the village. The phone box is on the corner
near Haverty's. Great craic going on inside. I push the phone
card in and punch the thirteen digits to reach Holfy's voice. Her
machine comes on, more soothing than any drink.

—It's me. I'm here—

She picks up.

—Here? Where's here? You're never here.

—Funny.

—I'm just in. I was stuck in the Holland Tunnel for—

—I love you.

—Yeah?

I smile. The American intonation mixed with her Icelandic gravel charms me even now. I have a pain in my stomach with yearning for her. A group stumbles out of the pub, roaring with drink. It's odd to see people drunk on the street. One of the women is pushing a pram, and yelling at her husband not to piss up against the wall.

—It's the locals out of the pub. It's noisy your end too.

—They're making another movie. I had to walk from Horatio with my equipment.

—Move away from the window. I can't hear you.

—I am away from the window. I'm in bed.

—In bed?

—On it. Want to do it?

We laugh the giddy, greedy laugh of happy lovers, rush to fill the precious silences to make the most of the call. There's a violent beating on the roof of the phone box. Rain, come thunderously without warning like the threat of a clenched fist.

—We need rain here. The humidity is worse since you left.

Finally, she asks about the funeral just as the phone pips. I give her the number and wait with an elbow on the cradle, the phone to my ear. Nothing but the fierceness of the rain belting down. The pubs are closed now, the streets deserted; lashed into silence by the sudden storm. Nothing but wetness. A car approaches; the glare of its headlamps catching me full in the face. Blackness. Slosh. Evidently, she can't get through. I decide to wait two more minutes. Shame whistles through the door and I hum to stop myself from thinking. My father is dead. The rain looks like it will go on forever. I'll wait until it ends. The phone rings, its loudness echoing.

—I'm sorry. A client called as soon as I hung up. She's a bitch. I had to take it.

—I want to be back with you. It's over with her. I've told her. Silence. Tiny international beeps. Tell her it's over.

—Holfy?

—I'm here.

—I want to be with you. I've told her I'm leaving.

I bite my lip on the lie.

—It's not my call.

—Fuck that. What do you know? We're at each other's throats. I can't help her.

—Don't leave her for me. Leave her for you.

—Such devastating fucking wisdom.

—I mean it.

—I am leaving her for me.

—I don't believe that.

I slam the phone down. Her voice goes on in my head. I hope she calls back to hang up on me. The rain has a grudging cease-less look at it. It's weakened, running noiselessly down the phone box. The phone doesn't ring. I rifle my wallet for a phone card but know already I used the last one. It feels like winter has slipped inside my coat. If Ursula is up, she might be worried. Still enough feeling left for worry, perhaps. I tear the cover off the telephone book to use as a hat and set off up the hill. At the top of the first steep rise, where the car stalls, I pause. I look out across the city. A scattering of higgledypiggledy goldenwhite lights that is Dublin. Lights sparkling as if they have nothing bet-ter to do than look magical. To the east, nothing but blackness, the scooped neckline of Dublin Bay and its seawaves washing up against the city. A ship far out in the bay. The tremendous noise of the sea slapping against Bray harbour, slapping too into the scoop of Sandycove, into Scotsman's Bay, into Dun Laoghaire pier where it washed clean over us that day and we kissing near the lighthouse, and across the bay; slapping its old song against Howth. And deep in the middle of its waters, away from the bobbing city, the sea is silent. The sea is nothing but silence. Silence and waiting. So much is hidden.

The light's on in the kitchen. I go up to the bathroom and dry myself, put on a dressing gown I haven't worn in almost two years, am surprised by the shortness of the sleeves. She's sitting there with a glass of brandy and a hot-water bottle cradled to her stomach. I can't bear the silence, the silence of last days.

—Any better?

—No. But no worse.

She manages to smile at herself, at me, at old quotes.

—You were out?

—Yes. It's pouring.

I look down at the floor, count the tiles. No lies. No lies anymore.

—I don't want to be scared walking down the street. I don't want to lose who I am to them.

She starts to cry; a horrible wail, out of her stomach, out of an untouchable pain. She rocks forward on the chair. I look away from her, at the russian doll. Too much said already. Say no more. Say no more. My hands tremble.

—Walk away. Walk away. You'll be walking away your whole life. Prick. You're a prick.

I close the door quietly through her screaming.

—Next time, ring her from here. Prick. You'll get your death of cold walking up that hill in the rain. What would the cunts of America do, then? You twofaced prick.

I go into the study. A crash. Another one. Flipflap of the cat door. Another crash. She starts to howl. I lie on the sofa and cover my ears. I leap up and run into her as she is hobbling to me.

—What do you want me to do, walk the street in search of them and kill them? It happened. There's nothing we can do. It's a sick place. It's life.

—It's not about that. Jesus you've got better—worse—at changing the subject. It's over. We've ended this so many times. Just go. You'll have your cut soon enough. Then go. Just go.

—Fuck the money.

Vomit jumps off the bed and goes out.

I wake to exhaustion. Darkness. For a horrible moment I wonder why the street is so quiet, thinking I am in New York. It's still night. Not a sound. Not even a gurgle from the water tank. £1,263 for his funeral. More money for Jennings. Great business, have to do nothing but wait. The garden sensor light comes on like a question; a black flash past the window; a light tink on the gutter. The birds are awake, waiting for something to happen. It's nearly six. I can't work out if it's morning or evening. At this time of year it could be either. The sky is untelling. A freight boat out in the bay, small moving lights offering hope like a thick delivery of post. A black flash startles me; I hold my hand up against the expected blow. But it's just a bird, diving. She lands, pecks amongst the foliage, traps a twig in her beak and rises up. Another tink and teeny scratchings as she finds her place; a flut-

ter, a coo of happiness. There's a perceptible lightness in the sky
but perhaps I'm adjusting to the night. No, it is morning; disc of
a sun, no bigger than a penny, slipping palely from the sea. Rising with regal deliberation. It was like this in the beginning. The
sun glints and is lost to the hopeless Dublin clouds. I lie down
again. We fucked like there was no tomorrow once upon a time.
Threw her prosthesis out the window one night because she
wouldn't turn around to me. What fun it all was. No more. No
more any of it. I turn over on my side. No more will her lap mold
itself into the elbow of my knees. I turn over on my other side
towards the back of the sofa and emptiness. No more will I smell
her after sleep. In Dorset Street, we had to do it just before eight
o'clock in the morning otherwise Mrs. Tweedy upstairs might
hear us. Of a weekday morning she'd be up and down to Mass in
St. Saviour's in Dominic Street. Ursula didn't want her hearing
anything and Mr. Tweedy off half the time with Mrs. Arkins from
Joseph's Mansions. We knew by the church bell we had to stop
and get up because she'd be on her way back with the *Irish Inde-
pendent* and twenty John Player Blue.

She is in the garden, weeding. The electric kettle is hanging
by its flex on the trellis. Cutlery is scattered on the lawn, a fork
stuck in the grass like a bizarre game. The wooden wine rack
caught in the bushes. Vomit is sniffing at the steam iron lying on
its wounded side. Wedding presents, all of it. No matter.

—You were on the phone to her last night.

—On the phone to whom?

She nods and keeps weeding.

—I don't care. Really. Do whatever you like. Out in the open.
Hide it. Whatever you like.

—I was out walking.

～　～　～

Her mother is the first to come. She doesn't bring Mulvany, for once tactful. Ursula and I are sitting in the kitchen with Muriel. The funeral was horribly quiet. No eager handshaking. I get up to put the kettle on. Muriel gets up too. Ursula's mother looks at me.

—They'll want sandwiches, she says, pushing the bag across the table. I look at her, at the bag; cheese, tomatoes, ham, mustard, bread, butter, lettuce. I start making sandwiches. Through the open window, my eye catches sight of the kettle hanging out of the fence. Go easy on the butter, Muriel says. You can tell he didn't pay for it. I concentrate fiercely on the job. This will all be over soon. Holfy: we will never be like this.

The hall door is shoved in, discreetly. Uncle Aidan. He puts his arms around me, the smell of stale cigarette smoke coming off him. Memory of Ruth. I try not to lean against his solid comfort. He holds me longer than I want and I feel myself stabbed inside. I push away from him.

—What are you doing here?

—Acting the fool. Is the tea on?

I look over at Ursula.

—You need a bit of makeup, he says, his voice going soft. Ursula laughs through a torn voice.

—That priest was full of shite. No offence anyone.

He lights up, looks for an ashtray.

—There's no smoking here, you.

—I'll go out, so.

He makes a face at Muriel and goes out into the garden.

We pile up the sandwiches. Aidan hisses at the cats, picks up the kitchen utensils and shouts in the window.

—I haven't ruined your garden installation, have I?

She looks out in the garden and shakes her head, laughing.

—Is it alright then if I bring in the kettle for a cup of tea before we're all parched?

He always has the right tone.

Nothing left here now. Nothing.

I visit Medbh and Brefini. They have television now, something they never believed in, that he never believed in his Trinity days when he was all *up the workers*. She mutes the sound on the box. They have another child whose name I don't know. I hand the single toy to Una.

—You're to share that with the baby.

—Her name is Hazel.

We all laugh except Una. She stares at me, a vagueness in her eyes, remembering me. She rattles the toy for sound.

—His name is Lamb Chops. He's on the telly in America.

She looks again at Lamb Chops and fires him in the corner. Little bitch, applerot of her mother's eye. Brefini cooks a bit of dinner and no one mentions Ursula. They are going to enroll Una in Irish dancing classes. Brefini plays the piano they've just bought so he can play and his daughter can dance along to it. I dislike them, a couple I've always liked. I drink most of the bottle of wine I brought and tell them funny stories about New York. Brefini offers to drive me home but I insist on a taxi to avoid any meaningful talk that Brefini might have planned. Standing up to go I see a face I know on the television. Medbh turns and looks at the screen and asks me what's up. It's Mr. O'Neill, the Taoiseach's press secretary, fat-faced, hurrying through a door. Have you not been following it, asks Medbh. He's great entertainment—one of the brown envelope brigade. Look at the scowl on him.

—He did my father out of money. I don't need a tribunal to tell me who he is.

I tell the taxi man to drive through town in the hope something will show me the Dublin I left. Nothing. The party's over. O'Neill in court. Maybe Da was right, what goes around comes around. Jesus. Becoming the father. Medbh is the great force in the home, Brefini relegated to husband, father, man to be organised. No intimacy between them. How utterly awful to be able to read the life of a couple. Like brother and sister. Maybe it gets that way with all marriages. I tell the taxi man to drive out to the old house in Irishtown. A light on and music. I'm tempted to ring the bell, tell them it's my house—my wife sold it without permission. Just to see their faces.

—Mister, are we sitting here all night?

—Dun Laoghaire.

—You want to go to Dun Laoghaire now?

—No. I want to go to Dun Laoghaire.

—No need to be smart about it.

We drive in silence. He'll talk. Eventually he'll talk. I can't think my own thoughts. I wait for him to talk.

—I got the mother-in-law drunk last night. And she a pioneer.

—Is that right?

—True as God. Injected the oranges with gin. She made a bit of a fruit salad after the dinner. She was hilarious with drink on her.

He lets me out at the pier.

I walk to the lighthouse and look out at the light sweeping the sky. I sit with my legs dangling over the edge. An icy wind blows in. Waves crash and slosh on the granite boulders. Foul sea. Foul wild sea. As good a time as any. The headlamps of a car shine on me.

—Are you alright there, boy?

The Garda Siochána come to pluck me from a wet death.

—Come on, so. Up out of that.

I go home and lie in bed. Imagine Holfy on me. Tonguing me; caressing me out of myself that first night. The shock when she punched me. Holfy knows who I am, what I am. Some women have the instinct of knowing men. Moments shatter. Ursula buying a flask for my father; bringing him up soup she made. His eyes on her; loving the switch to caring daughter-in-law. Knowing nothing of the people around his bed. His left hand is what I remember. Fingers black with nicotine. Lining up butts in the bedside locker in the hospital. The uncontrolled gurgling from his guts. Him falling into a stupor. Feeling death off him as tangibly as I felt it off Ruth. I should have talked to him. I felt sorry for him when I saw how terrified he was of dying. His face full of desertion. It took his fear for me to see him for something other than the misogynistic shit he was. But what use talking. There was never any understanding between us.

A truth that's told with bad intent beats all the lies you can invent. My last image of my life with Ursula is of the cats basking in hypnotic sunshine. Willy is sitting on the bonnet of the car. Vomit is stretched on a branch of the lilac tree. And Ursula is walking back to the hall door. A rather undramatic ending yet an ending nonetheless.

Desire

Even with Kennedy crammed the way it is Holfy is impossible to miss with the green tinsel around her neck. She is watching a man kiss a woman fleetingly, watching him take her hand and her baggage trolley and wheel away their lives. I envy them their easy affection.

She has cut her hair and dyed it a burnished copper. A new woman to get to know. No matter what wild thing she does she manages to look stylish. She should look older with short hair—like any older woman trying to look younger. She looks harsh. She has painted her fingernails green, white and gold.

—You look young enough to be my lover.

—You always look the wrong age. Good funeral, was it?

She has misunderstood. I was trying to compliment her but it came out wrong. I tell her about my father's funeral, about Ursula's decision to give me a cut of Bath Avenue, the new house in Dalkey, telling her honestly I felt caught.

—So you're rich. Good, take me to dinner. It took three hours to get to the airport to collect your ungrateful ass.

We go uptown to Café Luxembourg but I don't enjoy it. Holfy drinks a lot and I ask her what's wrong.

—Did you see your wife?

—You insist on calling her that. It's like an accusation.

—It's called reality.

—We met. She's fine.

—And?

—And nothing. I told her it's over, that we've ended it too many times before. She came to the funeral which surprised me but it shouldn't have. She never liked my father but she does have a fine sense of propriety. That's something I never liked in her—too many admirable qualities.

—Won't make that mistake again.

—Nope. Bitches like you all the way from now.

She laughs and I'm relieved. We have our banter again, our ease with each other. That night, in her bed I decide I like the haircut. I judge too quickly. She will always be more sophisticated than me. There are two kinds of people: those who can't balance sunglasses on their head and those who can. I must tell her this.

I wake up and am uneasy. It takes me a long moment to realise that Holfy is crying. She is sitting on the floor with her back to the bed, watching television. People are laughing on the television, drinking out of champagne glasses outside some brownstone. Holfy's laughter coming from the television. I look at the clock on the floor: after four in the morning. And now for Whitman, her voice says from the television. There she is. Like everyone else she is wearing a flapper-style dress. The video of her wedding. Robert is quoting Whitman. It's the first time I've seen it and seeing him with her, seeing them laugh together, turns me into an imposter in her life. I have never seen or heard her cry before. I put my hand on her stomach. Her crying worsens.

—It's so hard, she says.

—Yes.

She punches the mattress.

—I loved him.

I don't know what to say to her.

—I miss Robbie.

—It's past, I say. It's over.

She nods furiously; empty words of solace. It is not past—it's present. It's in her body.

It's not over. It's never over.

Do you know how it feels to lie in bed at four o'clock in the morning with your heart beating in your chest as if you had run a race and all it is, is fear you didn't ever love me. Do you know how deeply such fear strikes? My heart thumps so fast, I think it's going to stop, think it can't keep up with itself. Probably you feel that way when you're inside her. I don't know who she is but I know you're gone. I knew it when you came back for the funeral. Part of me wanted to do it with you. Stupidstupidstupid me. I

felt sorry for you because I knew you were upset because
he was dead and you were still angry with him. I could
sense her off you. I knew you'd put it into another
woman. You really know nothing. Or maybe you know an
awful lot. I opened to you, took you into me. Mornings at
my desk I would feel the cold dribble of you leak from me
and I would clench my muscles to hold you a moment
longer. I have learned something new. I have learned my
own hand. It's a far better lover than ever you were.

The rehearsed interest in your voice. You listened so
attentively to me. But your tone of voice talks deeper to
me than words ever can. I listened attentively, too. Three
thousands miles away and I heard it in your voice. And I
saw it in you, too. Saw you take the breath needed to say
the words. I heard the voice come up and out of your gut,
out of your tight throat. I saw you clutch the phone and
close your eyes and say I love you Ursula. You needed to
say my name. You never needed to say my name before.
Your words are hollow. Your words rattling and clanging
in a metal pail clattering on the cobblestones. I couldn't
be with another. I've never even thought of what another
man would be like. My eyes were never off of you. When
we parted in the morning at the end of Baggot Street, and
I turned the corner, I had to stop myself from looking
back. I knew you were still sitting there in the car, looking
at me and not looking for a gap in the traffic. I knew your
eyes were burning into me and wanting me to turn and I
never did. For ten years I never did. I felt, if I turned
around and looked at you the violence of my love would
be a gunshot. The traffic would screech to a halt, the
buses would stop coughing fumes. Baggot Street would be
hushed to silence; people would lean over O'Connell

Bridge and stare, dumbfounded, at an unflowing river. The gulls in the sky would stop crying and falling and rising up on the air and the grey sky would lighten and the rain would be switched off and people would stand there with awe-opened mouths at the buckling power of my love for you. And when I walked into the office and said Good Mornings and heard Good Mornings coated with *Isn't she nice but a little dull*, I would turn and look at them and their faces would drain of colour and the telephones would stop ringing and the faxes would stop sliding out and the photocopiers would go quiet, the air-conditioning would go quiet, the clocks would no longer tick on the walls, the watches on their wrists would no longer tick. My love, if I ever carried my love for you openly on my face, would have stopped the world from turning. My tremendous, unreciprocated, love.

What you have soiled for some other woman's *Yes*. Yes is the longest word. There is only one Yes. Yes screams with certainty. Yes is what you put on my finger in the chapel in Trinity College. Yes defines everything. Yes is the creation of love, of beauty, what we were. After the first Yes there are no other Yeses. After Yes, everyone else becomes a joyous No. You have made us a No.

The money from Bath Avenue is through. £144,000. They liked the sound of tennis. Imagine, they paid that and they didn't even see the roses in bloom. The price is a good omen—not only is the market on the up—144 is a Fibonacci number.

I'm selling the house in Dalkey as soon as it's finished. I'm getting good at getting rid of things. Daddy will be furious. I'm going to move into town. I hate the drive in, in the morning. It's so irritating—I just bought a fax so I

could get the copy in to them faster and now Fiona wants
me to work in the office. They prefer it—me typing it in
directly to the system. They want to see me earning the
shitty money. I've been paying too much in parking.
Everything. I won't bore you. Why am I telling you this?
I should rip it up. Fuck it—it's the last blast. She had
the gall to say it would be good for me with you away
and all that—getting in to the office and away from the
too quiet house. I'm sick of her. She commissioned an
article on International Women's Day and gave it to our
friend with the weeping crotch. Twofaced bitch. I'm
sending you back the 8 x 10s you sent me. It was sweet
of you to think of me but I really don't need photographs
to remember.

I'm sending you £55,000. That leaves me with £89,000.
It seems reasonable. I had to do it all; solicitors, estate
agents, the moving. Let me know if you object.

I'd love you to object.

Ursula.

I am inside Holfy, bruising myself against her creased arse and
thinking about Ursula. Imagining it is Ursula and she doesn't
want me and struggles but secretly she enjoys it. That weekend
we spent at her father's home; the shy way she bent away from
me; her hands gripping the mantelpiece; lifting her skirt; warm
pert buttocks against me; her father's laughter out in the garden;
shuddering at her cheeks brushing the curled hairs on my stomach. Only later realising the thrill for her was doing it in her
father's bathroom and I squirm at the odd relationship she had
with the man. The evening we spent in Searson's. Ursula noticing me noticing some skirt walk past. The moment is irretriev-
able. Neither of us pretend it has not happened. I am not the

kind of man to be tactless in that fashion and I bite my tongue for
the mistake. A marriage has many endings. We said nothing. The
first slip. Cracks in our lives we fall into; cracks become walls
around us. I curse and curse and Holfy comes and all the time it
is Ursula's back I am looking at in anger, it's her moaning I hear,
her cunt surrounding me.

I have been lying for years—telling myself I want this kind of
woman or that kind of woman. I want a woman I can fuck forever
but have been too afraid to admit it. Ursula is a paragraph out of
some feminist pamphlet. Holfy has changed my life. She fucks.
She likes my seed leaking out of her. Soft bubbling of her cunt-
farts afterwards. I was afraid of my wife's silent standard. The
standards in her eyes she could never hide. That night in Searson's I went and got us another drink and looked at Ursula in the
Smithwick's mirror. She was biting the end of a hangnail. I
thought then (and this was before we were married) I should
walk out now. The coward leaves a thousand times and never
leaves. Fifty-five thousand. About a thousand a month for every
month I put up with the conceited bitch.

Holfy is kneeling by the bath, rinsing the sides with the
shower nozzle. The bathroom is her temple: she keeps it immac-
ulate. It has a resolute order. The bath is half the size of an Irish
bath. Everything is bigger in America except the baths. I stoop
and push a finger inside.

—Stop it.

She is rinsing as if she is alone. I ignore her. She is always ready.

—No. Go away.

Her voice full of breathless work. She is sponging the sides,
chasing a long black hair clinging like a question mark on the
blue tiles. The hair resists like mercury. I lick her but she will

have none of it. Her hand reaches to stay upright and she slips. I am fully in before she even curses. I hold her hips firmly and wait for her acceptance. I can feel her planning. Nothing but a breeze in from the window. Footsteps on the sidewalk. A fit of coughing.

—Rape! she screams. The footsteps pause.

—Holfy, stop.

—Rapist!

I pull out.

She looks sideways at me, her eye a slit of anger turning to amusement. I pretend to be less shocked than I am.

—Now, she says.

I don't. Fear itself is both an attraction and repulsion. I get dressed and go out. The streets always offer solace. They are drilling on the highway. It's as if they are trying to break into my head. All my life I've been trying to prove to a woman what a man is without ever knowing what a man is. I've wanted to show the qualities that make a man wonderful. I have to stop caring about impressions.

Eventually I comply with Holfy's request. Part of me wanted to do it the first time she hit me but I pulled back. She explains it depends on the way it is done. We are playacting in bed, I slap her hard on her backside. There is no sound from her as if she is indifferent to my presence. I slap her again. She turns over and slaps me back, much harder than I thought she was capable of doing, harder than she would want. The insides of her thighs are wet with sweat. I kiss the redness, kiss the heavy thigh, kiss the leg, the back of the knee, search for pleasure with my fingers. Cut your nails. I go and cut them, change the music. I kiss her stomach. I'll never get my figure back now, she says. Her breasts are cold and heavy. She likes them oiled. Gentle soft caresses.

Sweet moans now. Her eyes are closing with the slow fondling. Her body is heavy with pleasure. She is lost in her own pleasure. I slap her harder. I keep hitting the same place and watch it redden. She makes no sound. She is stooped as if concentrating on something else. I hit her as hard as I can and my hand stings with the crack of skin. I am disgusted with myself, disgusted that I can hurt her this way and yet it is not enough. I can sense disappointment in her. It's worse than the time with the straps. It's a widening between us. She can enter my world but I cannot enter hers. She tells me to look away from her and the force of the punch knocks me off the bed.

I walk the streets, am forever walking the streets, looking at the painted advertisements, looking at the small ways the city changes. The Marlboro man has changed. The advertisement of the safe company has been there forever. A giant vault. A splendid trompe l'oeil of a safe opening. I stare at it for a long time to see how it deceives the eye. Words are useless. I can't get away from her. Nothing comes except words like anguish and heat and contempt. Hours spent doing nothing except replaying the worst moments of my life, trying to turn them into something they were not. Looking for redemption through recreating the past so that it shines, so there are no smudges. Go further, she says. When I go back to the apartment she is not there, a card on the kitchen table with a quarter glued to it. A photograph of a little boy on a fairground rocket. Fly to the moon is scrawled on it. I won't give up, this time I won't give up.

We are walking down Jane Street. The two huskies with the handkerchiefs tied around their necks are lying outside the flower shop. I stoop and stroke the green-kerchiefed one and she pets the red-kerchiefed one. She holds his head and shakes it vigorously. He growls and Holfy growls back.

—It was a good party.

She nods, holding the dog's snout in her clenched hands. He tries to retreat out of her grasp but she is holding him too firmly in her large hands. She looks at me disinterestedly, the large yellow and brown bruise still visible under her eye.

—Did you want to stay?

—Let's go home.

—No. Let's walk some more.

We walk down Gansevoort, down Washington and end up heading towards the Village. It's strangely quiet, the kind of night in Greenwich Village that I thought would happen a lot but it doesn't. Everyone is somewhere else. They are at films and plays and galleries and openings and restaurants. And, of course, they are working to pay the rent. But tonight, they are doing all of that somewhere else. There is little traffic. She buys some cigars in the Village Cigar. The first time I watched her smoking. It seemed so unpretentious in her hand. We are walking down a quiet residential street, brownstones on both sides. My life was an act for a long time, she says. She draws on her cigar. My life used to be improvisation. I look at her and wonder if she is being serious. But she goes on.

—Isn't that the way most people are? Living a life based on a kind of improvisation. An improvisation based on the fact that someone is watching the acting. Someone is watching how good we are at being ourselves when we are not ourselves at all?

—Only Catholics live like that.

—You say that because you are Catholic. If you were Jewish, it would be Jewish. The only way to live is to be selfish. Then you can give something to the world that the world might want. If you are both lucky.

We walk for a long time not talking. I am only aware we are holding hands and I am happy. We pass Cooper Union. It begins to snow, lightly, and as it falls we stop and look up at it, and because it is falling lightly, and it is windless and nighttime and lit up, the snow looks like it is falling from forever. It lands on our faces and melts gently on our warm skin and dribbles into nothingness. I squeeze her hand and tell her I feel more alive than ever I have. It takes practice, she says. We come upon a street full of stalls. Young people selling jewellery and scarves, woolly hats and sunglasses. The smell of hot food wafting from the other end of the street. We buy two hats with floppy ear covers. One red and one green. We would have to steal the huskies now. There are some people drug-dealing at the corner of Tenth and the easy manner of it shocks me. We go into the Lion's Head near Sheridan Square, a bar ruined by tourists like you, she says. This is the night I first have a vodka gimlet. Time slides into remembered first moments. It is one of those rare moments when we seem to forget everything, forget this insistence on living in the moment, the harshness, the impiety of sex, forget everything except the fat barman serving us.

She is sitting on the sofa reading the *Paris Review*. She has her feet up on my lap. She is absorbed in her reading. I pour her some fresh coffee and she uhms. A small icy part of me wonders if we can live a life together. I feel this horrible need for a commitment and try and push it away from me. I know this will be as much as it ever will be with her. Today we are together. Yesterday we were together. That is all. Nothing more than that. Tomorrow does not exist. It doesn't exist in art so it doesn't exist in life. She has never said that to me but I know it is who she is. It is how she lives. She lives in this moment alone. I sit in front of her and wait until she looks up at me:

—What?

—Nothing.

She goes back to the *Paris Review,* looks up at me again. She takes off her spectacles.

—What is it?

—Nothing.

—It wouldn't work. You know it wouldn't. Christ, I don't know. It just doesn't fit.

I get up and get dressed for the winter outside.

—We promised to be straight up. I'm being straight up.

I zip up my jacket and agree with her.

—Being straight up is what we said we would always do.

—Do you really want—

—O please shut up.

The streets are busy with shoppers. Happy Holidays. I long for Ireland where no one will be offended if you say Happy Christmas. I'm tired of it all. For so long I thought Holfy was attached to me. That she had all these elaborate defences. In the grocery store I hear a camera click. Some promotional people are taking photographs. I wander around the store and have no idea what it is I have come for. The sound of the camera shutter is all I hear. I stare at the shelves in the hope that I'll see what it is I want. I feel as if I am a shoplifter and try to force purpose into my bearing. But in the end I give into the clicking camera. I see Holfy setting up the shoot we did last week and I am trying not to look so impressed. She is eating biscuits and smoking and trying not to drink coffee. We are on the roof. She tells me that professional photography is about knowing that the accident will always happen if you take enough shots. It's about knowing that the best shots have only a little to do with skill and a lot to do with patience and spontaneity. Look at Cecil Beaton. The most boring photographer in the world. How can I help you? a voice asks. I am smiling at a rack of Italian wine and the shop assistant asks me again how he can help me. I look at him and can't help but stare at an inflamed boil over his lip. The camera is still clicking. I tell him I'm fine and when he goes back to the counter I take the first bottle I see under eight dollars. Nice region, he says. I nod and look at his eyes and then at his hand offering me the change. The photographer is putting in a new roll of film. I want to tell him not to waste too much film on the shots. There is no spontaneity in an unopened wine bottle. She is right what she says about the self.

The man behind the counter doesn't give me a bag. Can I have a bag, I say. What? he says. A bag. Can I have a sack? Sure, he says. I feel I lose more of myself with the addition of each American word: sack, trash, mail, sidewalk, store, highway. I am becoming America with these words. Words are all I am. I know this because I am in silence now. I have been in silence for all this time and I have not existed. We exist only when we speak. The geraniums are beginning to fade. Some of the leaves have turned a translucent beige and crack between my fingers. The healthy leaves give off their pungent smell. Geraniums smell of hopeful summers and suddenly I know myself as well as I know the smell of these flowers. I got a package from Medbh today. A six-pack of Club milks. I open one with my tea. Peel off the yellow wrapper. Then the foil. The remembered taste of the chocolate. It begins to rain hard and I feel overcome with sadness for a lost Dublin. It rains hard all day and starts to thunder. Lightning flashes whitely in the sky and I can no longer fool myself into thinking I am home. But Dublin is not home. How stupid of me to slip. I make more tea and pick up the letter again.

Inside the darkroom. The brutish honesty of the words. When I describe something inaccurately the words sit there, leaden and smug. Suddenly I am no longer pitying Ursula. Ever since we ended I thought of her as the vulnerable one. Such a lack of insight is impressive. The wind has taken up, and the leaves on the trees fight with it. I bite into another Club milk. I chew it tastelessly. I wipe some crumbs from my lips and am surprised by tears on my face. I wipe them off as if they belong to someone else. My eyes burn. I say my mother's name aloud and I remember being in bed with her and holding her and she was telling me it was alright. There was no bogeyman going to get me. She would take care of me, she would. I was shaking and snivelling and she took the edge of the sheet and said blow and I blew my nose in the sheet and she said Lord Jesus that nose of yours is full of yuckies and I looked up at her and she made a disgusted face and I burst out laughing and she said I'm not washing that sheet because it will only attack me, and I am lost in her eyes. There is no safeness anymore. There's just myself and the long memory of my mistakes. But I don't want to end up like the ones who do not speak. The ones who sit and say nothing and pretend to be nice but are operating. Always gathering information and never giving. I don't want a dry and cynical life.

I leave a wad of writing by Holfy's bed with a note.
Please read. Be honest.

She writes a note on the bathroom mirror:
Like there is an alternative to honesty pour moi?

I have what I think is a common affliction: I want to be liked. It makes for both bad writing and uncomfortable living. I writhe inside myself. I don't always behave in a nice fashion. I am sometimes arrogant, but this, more often than not, is because I am reacting against the tendency to be nice. My own company puts me on edge. When I come home, and close the door behind me and sit in the friendless silence I am afraid of what feels like the presence of God. I have vague memories of myself as a child playing on the road. I am alone, building a dam in the gutter to stop the rainwater from running into the shore. I remember my mother calling me for my tea and not wanting to go because my game was too exciting to leave.

One of the traits trailing behind courteousness is a pretence of stupidity. I think it is particularly true of my class. To nod and affect ignorance. To hide intelligence like stolen goods, as if thought is segmented by class. The brain runs and runs and runs.

Words leave me. They grow tired of banging around in my head, arriving at no sense. There was a time when I knew exactly what I thought but those thoughts no longer belong to me, they belong to a past that no longer exists. For a long time I had the instinct of a streetwise child but I have lost that common sense. I have pretended to be clever. I made the mistake of wanting to seem intelligent to some unknown reader. A reader who read so much and who understood so much that unless I was superb, would raise an eyebrow in weary disappointment.

What I have discovered is that I am lost. I am looking at myself in utter bewilderment. Whatever it is, it is unfathomable to believe in the love of God. How can a child understand God? God waited, as God always waits.

You have to go deeper. What you say to me in the quietness of the night when we can't sleep. Your voice, that's the voice of the writing—this is nonsense. This *I* you write about. Who is in your sentences. Who are you trying to please? Be as self-ish as a cat. That's the kind of writer you are, or, I should be more accurate, it's the kind of writer you could be. Grip me by the throat and hold me until my face reddens. Otherwise you lose me. If you lose me I will never pick it up again. Do anything in my company but never bore me.

I drop the wad of paper on the bedside table. It had only taken her seven pages. I want to marry Holfy. I write in her darkroom. It's the only place I can forget I'm living in Manhattan. Botero sits under the lamp, saliva dripping from his jowls. Holfy has asked me to write a story cutting into the weave of love and sex but nothing is happening. I want to go and make more tea but it is too early. I look at the rest of her note.

Forget about understanding death. My husband. Your sister. Your father. We do not have death in common. We have grief and life. Death lives on its own. Forget your sister. Every time I touch you I know Robert approves and if he did not I would not care. There is nothing to learn about death except that it is not living. Stop looking for meaning. Go back to the writing. When you know what's going to happen in the next sentence stop. Stop. If the writing is not a mystery to you, you are writing dross. Make up your mind whether you want to write or type. Put Kahlo into the novel and call her Zoe. People need symbols. Put everything in it that people want and then cut the head off the expectation. Break the rhythm. Annoy. Make sure no one ever likes you. Never be accused of writing a smooth sentence. Smoothness is a soporific. Write about our love with unflinching honesty. Yes, I know you have little respect for honesty that doesn't flinch. Perhaps you know this already but you don't know what it feels like. You don't know the meaning of the pleasure in pain. You don't understand the joy of bruises. Bruises frightened you in the beginning. Sadomasochism is the most brutal acknowledgment that you are alive and that you can humble yourself before God. If ever you go as far as I want you to go with the writing, you will learn that God is sitting on the parapet in Gansevoort Street, waiting for your screams. And She is smiling.

Holfy should be the one doing the writing. Sometimes, when I'm working, I put my face in my joined palms to think and I smell her there, rising out of my skin, as once I smelled Ursula.

So much time spent not writing, sitting there wanting it written. Wanting words to flow, wanting some blossoming story to come out of the past. But instead my mind tramps through old memories, I retell myself old humiliations, rewording them, reshaping them so they end the way they should have ended. I sit there staring at the wall, wondering when the pain will ever go away, and life will start to unfold as I know it is meant to unfold. I tell myself there must be a plan right here in this room, and somehow I am avoiding it.

Do you remember the lake in Pennsylvania? I warned you about the snapping turtles. Remember the stillness on the lake? Remember your glasses fell out of the rowing boat. We were drinking vodka gimlets and the homemade margaritas without the ice. It was sunny, and we let the boat drift, and we dozed, and there was a gentle thud when we hit the bank and you were jittery in your sleep because the leaves brushed your face but you didn't waken. I turned and woke you because I wanted you, and you said you missed Ireland, and you hated missing it, and I said shut up. Come here, I said. The clumsy rock of the boat and the fierceness of your fingertips. Soft fucking. Balance your sentences with arrogance and indifference. Put commas in the wrong place. This is our story and syntax will not hold it. It belongs only to you and me. Are you understanding what you have to say? I am considerably older than you. Trust me. Never help the reader. Refuse to accept that you have to explain anything. Do not care if they get to the end of the paragraph. The paragraph belongs only to us.

Assume no one will read this. It is the only way to write.

Remember what your sister said to you before she died. And the dead become more and more right with the silent yawn of time. You rest on the weakest sentence. Your only charm is your pretence of sophistication. Write the story and make sure there isn't a single line of fantasy in it. Danger lies in the truth. Write only what happened between you and me. It has to be as clear as a photograph—as clear as one of *my* photographs. The photo I took of you that day at Shelter Island. That's not me, you said. You were wrong, it was you. It's the you that you go to bed with, isn't it? The years will make you that photograph. You and I are perfect devils. Avoid lies, especially if they seem necessary for plot. There is no plot. People sense lies. Lies curl and create ugliness like paper peeling off a damp wall. The greatest pleasure in death is that there will be no more arguments. The heart, when it stops beating, smiles. Open your legs and let me see you. I had forgotten your smell. Nature is so clever. Men are so sweet when they're excited. Read me something by Yeats.

Never give all the heart.

Indeed. Never have children. If you have children you will have to grow up and that would disappoint me. Don't go back to teaching—it sucks the marrow from your soul and your wisdom fades into the brick brains of those who can not learn what they do not know. Teaching is a wall falling into a vermilon sea. What I like most about you is your yellow flaring laugh and it lashing joyfully against the wind of your anguish. The first time you saw me naked and you asked me

where did I get such a happy bottom and I said I grew it
myself. I knew it would be good then. I never tire of your
tongue. Such soft licking. People like driving on roads that
are lined with trees and they like to see a bird flash across
blue sky. If you take away the blue sky they will despise you.
Do you know what we mean by happiness? Arriving back at
the car and not having a parking ticket. Excitement is night-
clubs and movies and getting drunk and watching children
play sports badly and learning to be sophisticated with
people who do not know the meaning of style. Excitement,
then, is stepping into the artifice of adrenaline and knowing
we can step out again and return to the familiar smell of the
ugly boxes we call home. I do not want people to know about
our life in Gansevoort Street.

Sadomasochism is the deepest form of love. It goes
beyond any basic understanding of cathexis. Age matters.
We think we can move beyond it but we cannot. People want
to know how old you are before they sleep with you. As if
approval is buried in years. People are like trees—you can tell
their age only after they have fallen. The Sunday we cut
down the lilac tree that was cracking the cement with its
weight. I could never imagine sitting there looking at the tips
of the Twin Towers without the lilac tree but of course I did
get used to it. Everything changes. We get used to it all or
shrivel.

There is only one thing I miss. No more will you kiss me
and make me breakfast. How I loved the sound of you in the
kitchen and your dreadful singing. How you loved the precision of the coq removing the egg tops. Nothing compares to

you cooking for me. Such things make life bearable. You know less than when I first met you. This is the only sex that is possible between us now. Paper sex.

The night I came back from Brooklyn and the stereo was blaring in the apartment and you had all the strobes on and the fish lights flashing on the back wall and you were dancing on your own and it was a you I had never seen.

You would never dance in public. You said it told too much, the way people move to music. I knew that night that you would leave. Not then, not immediately, but there was something trapped in you that I hadn't noticed before and watching you move to the music with Grace Jones I knew it: could sense our ending with the certainty I sense when a movie is ending. You wanted me to need you. The only thing I didn't need was your need. I grew up in the sixties. You confused me with Jackie Kennedy's generation.

Here is how I want you to end it:

At the street fair in Little Italy. We are at Florent's show and we are sitting on a stoop and eating bratwurst. There had been a street fair. We had our fortune told. We had shot the plastic bears with water guns. We went into the empty church and there was an elderly couple sitting there with a life-size pink panther sitting between them and for once I didn't take the shot even though I could have got it with the Leica. They got up then, she with the toy under her arm as if it were a tired child, and we kissed for a while in the church and when we came out, the fair was getting noisy. People everywhere. Cops smiling. We walked down through the Village. We kissed in a doorway in Perry Street.

You want to capture my essence but you should know—
even at this stage of your life—to *know* is impossible. You are
a mystery to yourself so how can you know me. Women and
men are railway tracks racing away in the distance, never
meeting.

Holfy didn't always speak with certainty. She had a way of
talking, of asking questions, that made her sound neither rhetor-
ical nor challenging. What I remember most of all was her hesitation. Is it Monday? Somewhere. Her tone was full of questions.
When we were on the roof and having breakfast, she would start
to go into what she felt the writing needed and as she talked I
would watch the pigeons land and collect branches and fly across
the street and build their nest over Judd's Gym, and all the time I
would know that she had an uncanny way of leading me into
myself. On these rare mornings when the phone didn't ring, she
would speak and I would listen and it was as if God was placing a
hand on us. But when she did break through her indecision, when
she grew impatient with my mistakes, her voice rang like a bell
on a clear day. It was impossible to argue with her then. I would
go back to the writing and stare at it with contempt, as if it were
toying with me, as if I were not responsible for the words I had
typed that morning. So I would go back to the daisy wheel and
type it again. Go back again. The sound of that machine always
made me feel like I was working. That an honest day's shilling
was being earned for an honest day's work, as my father would
say. The only thing that is more important than writing is the
confirmation that it is work. This is why publication matters. She
could always read where I was going before I understood that I
was making the journey at all.

❧   ❧   ❧

The apartment is quiet. Botero is lying under the unmade bed, wagging his tail limply, eyes empty of hope: I never feed him morsels. I stick my head out the open roof window. Holfy is lying sunbathing on the roof. She is wearing the dark brown one-piece and she turns and talks—she has someone with her. A woman wearing a violent pink bikini. A tray of drinks sits on a chair between them. A strange silence between them: not the spent, drunken lethargy of sunbathers.

—Hello, I say, voice so bright it might crack the ice in their glasses.

Both women look up and smile. The pink bikini is wearing mirrored sunglasses. Holfy holds out her arms for a kiss. I stoop and do not meet her lips—my kiss touches her forehead. She runs a hand lazily down my leg:

—You remember Magda.

—He remembers me.

I nod a perfunctory smile in her direction and her mouth smiles back. I am careful not to stare at her body: it gloats, it is so well toned.

—Three Pimm's do you think, sweetheart?

—Why not?

I make the drinks, dunking the cucumber slices beneath the ice. So much is said with the flash of an insincere smile. I rest the glasses on the window ledge and stroke Botero. The unmade bed. My stomach tightens. Without thinking I spit generously into the Hungarian's glass. We smalltalk awhile. Holfy mentions dinner twice. But I've begun to dislike this dark bitch far too much to sit and eat with her. Magda asks me how my day was, in

a vile parody of domesticity. She is a woman who asks questions
either for direct information or else, as now, for self-amusement.

—It's not a trick question, she says to my hesitation.

—Magda is a photo editor, sweetie.

I look at Holfy blankly and then at Magda who is smiling as if
I am missing a punch line.

—My day was horrible.

They burst out laughing. The Hungarian slips her fingers
inside her bikini bottoms and smoothes the fabric. A pigeon
lands and collects a twig off the roof; drops it flying across the
road; flies back; picks another. I pull myself out of the adirondack
and wave them goodbye.

—Call Florent? wonders Holfy to my back. I ignore her. She
has recovered from the dead cat it seems. I do some work and try
to dismiss the quiet hum of their conversation and burbling
womanish laughter. I look up from the worktop, understanding
what it is I hate about this Magyar: her self-assurance. She is the
kind who comes to the city and can take it on; become even
more sophisticated than New Yorkers themselves. She has
tapped American naïveté and I am ludicrously jealous of her success. I go to my desk and write. Achieve nothing. I sit there,
elbows on the desk, head in hands, fed up with it all. Holfy drapes
over my shoulder, cooing in my ear. Smell of suncream and
Gitanes off her.

—Come talk to us.

She is as angry with me as I am with her but she is making an
effort; she has not forsaken the night when the Hungarian will be
gone.

—She's having a difficult time. She's divorcing. She's married
to a shit. He works in that nuclear plant?

—Henri works in a nuclear plant.

—Not Henri. Istvan—her husband. He's a pig.

—How sad.

—Don't. She's a good woman.

—Right.

—I'll call Florent. What do you want?

I shake my head despite the hunger.

—You *are* a sulker.

She gets food for three anyway. The two women eat on the roof. I give up pretending I will write and lie on the futon in the corner. It's on the stroke of eleven. Nearly six in Dublin. The Angelus coming on the radio. Mother. Used to be putting the dinner out on the table then. Liked that time of the evening with her. Does she ever think of us. Sure. There's not a day that passed. Never give her the chance to say that. Never. Quiet outside now. I write another letter to Ursula, another letter I will write and leave in the drawer. Life is quiet without you. No matter how I fill my days and nights the absence of you haunts me. My gut is wrenched with the loss of you. When I went back to Dublin I knew it was over for you. I could see the calmness of a decision made in your eyes. I made every mistake possible. If it had been the other way round I would have laughed to put you at your ease. But not you. You were a laser beam of directness. Everything swirled in confusion. I had fallen in love with your directness. You could fight your own battles and if you did not always win the argument, your dignity made it seem so. Your directness was chopping up any morsels of love I put on the table before you . . . I tear it up. I have to stop. Have to stop and go on. You'll marry out if you marry her my father said. And my father was right. I am falling still. The pebble falling over the cliff.

Falling into blue falling into the blue and still I don't move in the heat in the sun I don't move and there is a train going past, heavy rattle and thud of it going past and Daddy is walking between the seats and saying he'll be back in a minute and Ruth is asleep and I'm on my own and everything is going past in the train in the blueness and he mightn't come back and there was that time we were going to Galway and I was thinking I made a mistake in marrying you and it was forever and I had made my bed and that was it and the train is going past rocking and rocking and still I stay here and I'm falling into the blueness and still counting the carriages as they pass under the bridge, hoping for that next kiss.

Laughter from the television wakes me.

—Can you lower that a bit?

She ignores me.

—Can you please lower the television a bit?

—Yes, I can lower the television. As much as I want. I'm lowering nothing. This is my apartment.

Her apartment. Right. When I wake again music is playing. Bartók. How quaint. I sit up in the bed, and, although I can't see them in the darkness, I know what I knew instinctively since I came in earlier. The apartment is soaked in their sensuality. I see myself as the halfarsed Urbanite I am, as Holfy must see me; as the Hungarian, with the unerring exactitude of the stranger, sees me; as Ursula must have seen me when I came in soaking wet after ringing Holfy. All the lies swim about me; shoals of fish; the first time I heard myself lie to my father about the money I had stolen from his wallet to buy the Meccano set; the time I heard

Ruth lie to my father about where she had bought the meat for dinner (and she knew I, small as I was, knew she was lying); my father lying that it was work kept us late when it was him stopping at Mrs. Marjoram's on the way home; all the countless, unnecessary lies I told and continue to tell. I pick up the keys. Holfy laughs at some whispered comment and her laugh, her entrancing laugh, disgusts me. As I pass them in the darkness an arm reaches out to me, touches me:

—Come to bed.

Her voice contains no hint of Magda by her side. My heart is full of hate but instead I take up her hand and kiss her fingers; the ruby ring Robert bought her; my lips touch her skin for the last time. I think of her feet; the tanned hard skin she loves me to caress when she is tired. Her perfect arches. The tip of a lit cigarette glows as Magda inhales beside her. The lurid smell of sex. This is her life. This is her real life, tonguing this bitch. I am the present hobby. In the kitchen I fiddle with the key ring to remove keys and then give up. I have always held on to keys. Holfy's. My father's. Medbh's. The house in Ireland. Botero charges out after me when he hears the door chimes ring and she shouts after me:

—Some cigarettes, please?

I pause to search for irony: something she will take to her grave but nothing comes. One day I will come up with a parting shot for someone. The dog looks up at me and then to his leash:

—No. Go in. Go in.

He looks up, sad eyes on him. I get a tub of yoghurt out of the fridge and he dances on his hind legs with excitement. I take the lid off and put it on the floor.

—Happy birthday, Bo.

He slurps messily and I leave before he finishes.

The gate is closed where we park the car. I bang on it with the keys. Lazy flickers from the Chinaman's hut, he is watching television. I bang louder, loud enough for him to hear me. I will be glad to see the back of him. A prostitute, resembling a weary Aretha Franklin, drifts along the sidewalk.

—Want in, honey?

Nothing more seductive than a nigger offering. Always wondered what dark meat would be like. Brown and purple, a strange combination. When I turn to look back he has already clopped past, his hands flicking up his orange miniskirt; shining black buttocks. He pauses without turning then walks on, bored. I wrap the gate and kick it. A light goes on. Chinky drags himself out of his chair and hits the button on the wall. He spits on the ground and I salute him.

—Hot night.

He ignores me as always.

—Where she?

—She come.

We are three feet from each other in the elevator. He reeks of cigarettes. He stops the elevator and walks in the general direction of the car; senses I have already spotted it; turns back to the elevator; waits. I turn the ignition and Janis Joplin comes on. Holfy's cassette. *Get it while you can.* She could always push it further than me: that is her sin; that is the only sin. The car is tight between wall and pillar. Chinky watches, waiting for me to damage something. For two years I have wished this bastard a good morning and for two years he has looked at me the way he is looking at me now. I manoeuvre it out and drive into the elevator beside him. We drop slowly. This is the first purposeful thing I have ever done. We jolt to a halt. The exit gate rattles up. I reach into my wallet and take out a twenty. Already he is walking away. I call after him. He looks at me—at the tip—with passionate disinterest. He turns back to his hut. I go after him and stop him and offer him the money again. He looks up at me and for the first time I see him closely; he is alert and full of disgust. His breath is nauseating. I crumple the money in my fist and punch him full in his face. He falls back a step but holds his balance. Blood dribbles from his nostril. He smiles and turns to his office. I run like fuck, hit the down button on the gate and jump in the car. The gate starts to rattle down in front of me. I shoot out onto Little West Twelfth and almost hit a man pushing a falafel stand. I spin around onto Gansevoort and stop for a second. I can't resist. I turn the car lights off and double back. He has his back to me with a gun in his hand pointing at the sidewalk. I reverse and make for the West Side Highway. I always imagined that whenever I left this city it would be up along the Hudson River. I take the Lincoln Tunnel and feel freedom in the breeze rushing through the open windows. The last time I'll have to put up with her age-thickened arse, her padded bras.

I have to get past hatred. I think of God, the last refuge of the hopeless. Is God happy? God must be bored watching the same unimaginative mistakes repeated and repeated and repeated.

Unravelling

I drive west for dead hours. I feel nothing except the coffee weakening with the miles. The traffic has long since thinned but never stops. Morning seems centuries away. Trucks pass, their roar more ferocious, more urgent in the humid night. For three hours there hasn't been a single bend in the road. My eyes are heavy with sleep and my anger at her has receded, diluted to an impotent impulsiveness and a road going to I don't know where. I turn the radio off and stare ahead into the miles. America is a highway, going nowhere. Each time I think I am doing fine, changing the rules, changing myself, but I am doing nothing but making the same mistakes, can no longer see the truth in anything.

The car hits gravel on the shoulder and the noise jolts me awake. I take the next exit. Four in the grimy morning. I pull up at the back of a closed Dairy Queen. My eyes are burning and gritty. I let the seat back and sleep.

Birds wake me. It's five—not yet bright. I drive back to the intersection to get on the interstate and then swing around and stop in the roadway, the engine idling. Enough of straight roads. I put the car into gear and drive back past the Dairy Queen. Night has not yet left the truck stop. The Iron Skillet. All food all day. Yummy. Even though people are eating greasy breakfasts and the sky is haunted with a pallid blueness, night clings to the restaurant; sticks to weary cigarette butts in unemptied ashtrays, to the tired eyes of the waitress slouching towards me with coffee sloshing in its pot; it creeps out of the sullen silence of the jukebox. Groups of dungareed men slumped on orange plastic chairs around large tables drinking coffee and smoking. They could be farmers if they weren't so lethargic. I look for a table without a phone but they all have them.

After I order breakfast I stare at the phone, look away from it, look back at it, give up and punch in the code. It takes three tries to get it right and then I hang up before she answers. I have no stomach for breakfast and know I have to phone her.

—Mm?

—It's me.

—Mm. Hi me.

—Can we talk?

—Mm.

—Will you please wake up? Is she still there?

—Mmm.

—I'm calling from a truck stop.

—Mmm?

—I'm calling from Pennsylvania.

—Is it fun?

—It's over.

—Pennsylvania's over?

—We are.

—We are. Really?

—I've had enough.

—You only know when you've had enough when you've had too much.

—Magda is too much.

—What a squirrel you are. Ciao.

—I'm serious.

—You're calling me from a truck stop in the middle of the night to say it's over, yes? I've got a job to get up for in three hours. You tell me it's over? Good luck. What do you want me to say, don't do it? Well, Serious, hope you're not in my car. I need it for the job in New Jersey this morning.

—I am. I can't explain it. I have to be by myself.

—You don't *have* a self to be with. Fuck off. Are you in my car?

—Yep.

She hangs up and I listen to the buzzing of the telephone line for a long time. I look around, sure the diners know she has hung up on me, and when the waitress comes with my plate and raises her eyebrows, she raises them not to ask me to make room for the plate, but to tell me I deserve to be sitting here with a telephone in my hand and no one talking and no one listening. Two blacks stuffing their faces at the other end of the restaurant. My

stomach lurches at the sight of the food. A train passes, wailing.
The same cry as ships in Dublin Bay on a foggy night. At the
cash desk my eye catches sight of a poster on the dirty yellow
wall behind the waitress: *Nothing can ever change the fact that you and
I once had wonderful times.* Only in America. Holfy got fat and I
couldn't bear the sight of her fat. There must have been a
moment when love stopped, a clock giving its final tick, the sea's
final ebb. I didn't want go grow old with her. No nice way of
saying it. I walk out into the parking lot and look around at
America. I can't remember which direction is which. Her impla-
cability, that, more than anything, is what I'm driving away from.
I go back into the truck stop and get a pack of cigarettes out of
the machine. Four weeks since I put one in my mouth. I tear the
cellophane wrapper off. No ceremony. The tip is fatter than I
remember. I cough, and, even with the unpleasantness of coughing, a calmness fills me and I feel violently alive.

Dazed and drunk with heat. A bird flashes across the front of
the car. A soft pop like a Styrofoam cup splatting flat. I pull over.
A mush of feathers and innards. I park off the highway under an
oak tree and sleep. I wake sweating and parched. The windscreen
is covered with drips of sweat from the oak leaves. Even the trees
are weary of the heat. Rain comes then stops as quickly. Birds
peck at the earth. Lilac smells stronger after rain. I never knew
what pleasure was until Holfy took me in her soft mouth. I light
a cigarette. Sweet identity a cigarette gives. A For Sale sign at the
edge of the road: Ayn Runnings. Everything she touches turns to
Sold.

The terrors come as fiercely in the day now. Hungry fat crows
waiting to devour. America is a highway with no exits. Meaning-

less highways stretching into infinity. I can't bear another night in the car. I stay at a Fairfield Inn in Sioux City. The Fairfield Inns, the Taco Bells, the Amoco filling stations: the roads of America; a litany of anonymity spread across a continent. The cattle in the early morning fields, their hides black and steaming in the haze, cantering like circus horses in the heavy morning. I pass through Wahoo. Wahoo Wahoo. An owl calling. I keep driving. Holfy is sliding into a past with Ursula. Ruth is dead. Father is dead. I had felt sickly free at his funeral, like a door had been unhinged by a fierce wind. I had thought of my last name, my father's name, and that I was the last child to carry it. After my own death there would be no one, no one would carry the name.

L o n e   T r e e

I like it here. The space. The realtor looked nervous, shocked that I agreed to buy the barn so quickly. There's a small house too but it was the barn that attracted me. The place had been unsold for years. I know why Holfy was apprehensive that night I got back from Dublin. It wasn't Ursula. It was the freedom the money from the house gave me. I had choice now and Holfy sensed I would be looking around, looking for a freedom she couldn't give me. Ursula's voice is leaving me at last. All the voices are leaving me.

On the distant highway, a car shimmers past. American cars have a way of being, a sense of movement that suggests their destination is unimportant; their function is to make the highway exist. Here, far from the cities, beneath a vast blue sky, cars are alien; an ugliness cruising across the plains. When I go into Lone Tree, people's faces appall me; the pain of their lives glares like pornography. The isolation has made me too sharp an observer of misery. I need the starched blue sky I can run off into. A sea without wetness. Everything is bigger here. All the voices are nearly gone. Finally, life started when I left Holfy.

I have lost interest in working on the barn. At least temporarily. It's too hot to work and it seems blasphemous not to be having fun on Independence Day. I am sitting on the broken porch. There is no breeze. The kitchen is the only place with an air conditioner and I move in there. The cicadas, the cacophonous cicadas, are screeching Ursula's name. I see her walking away from me. Now, after the parting, her walk has an alienated majesty about it. I sit in the grim kitchen and read the book about the Baird murder that took place a mile away, some years ago. It's badly written but I am hooked on the sloppy and conceited writer who is giving, as he puts it, a dispassionate and unbiased account of one of America's most baffling murders. Whenever a writer claims to be impartial you can be sure he'll be falling over himself to hide his little opinions, and a stupid writer, like this one, will fail. I wake with the book on my lap and the heat of the sun coming through the dirty windowpane. I'm looking for the reason why, with the answers dancing around me, I haven't changed. The birds begin to compete with the cicadas, singing the night in. I drag myself up and begin drinking, drinking myself into stupor. Happy freedom of drunkenness. Mosqui-

toes in the house again. Waiting for me to go to bed to eat me.
Fuck this country. A vodka gimlet. A loud bang across the fields
sends a shiver through me. The Baird couple dead on the floor in
front of me. Even the worst scribbler can set the mind racing. In
the black sky a ball of light climbs slowly into the sky, opens and
scatters its beauty, a cascade of reckless jewels fading away into
darkness. Moths bash off the screen searching for an opening.
There are no shortcuts. Only a sparkle ago I had my arm around
Holfy's waist and she had her arm around mine and we were leaning against the bridge along the Hudson River with thousands of
others, watching the fireworks until we grew tired of the oohs
and aahs and our necks hurt with looking up and we started kissing because we looked at each other and felt the same thing;
luckiest people in the world to be together. Once upon a time, a
long moment ago, I was down by the pond in Dublin, leaning on
a bridge with Ursula, waiting for the train to go under and counting the carriages and writing down the number and we'd kiss if
we agreed on the same number. Go home and study if we got it
wrong. Waiting for the train to go under and we were so happy
we didn't think gravity could keep our feet on the ground. I am
twisted with anger at the stupid bastard I was with her. And with
Holfy. If only she had put up with a little foolishness from me.
Put up with me, my mind whispers into a dead past. I am jealous of
our past, of her present without me. God must have been this
jealous when Eve and Adam first set eyes on each other.

Perched on the listing porch with the vodka and mug of ice,
the ice melting with the night heat before I've reached the end of
the drink. There is no forever, only the eternity of our little
beginnings and littler endings. I finish the drink with its melted

ice giving it a faint taste of wet cardboard. If I hadn't got that call
from Gerry. If we hadn't bought that house in Bath Avenue. But I
am lying to myself. The hardest lies to get past are my own. *If*
does not exist. What happened? Nothing happened. Everything
happened. What happened was I fell and didn't see the fall.
Ursula's heart was no longer in it. She saw it long before me. I
thought we were finding a new beginning. The night we were
having the house warming before we sold it. I had called it a
house cooling and she hadn't laughed. We told no one we were
selling as soon as it was finished in case the word would get out
that we were being driven out. I wanted to make it a special
evening, to tell people it was a symbol of our commitment to
each other. But even then she was long past me. A chipmunk
darts out of a crack in the porch. His tail flicks, bobbing in tan-
dem with his fat-cheeked cheeping. He is full of nervous happiness for summer. My mind drifts around Ursula, around Holfy.
Holfy never wore T-shirts. And she never let me wear them. The
necks are disgusting. The tiniest things bonded us, made us
insoluble. The way she glanced at me and her irony flashed off a
roomful of people and landed on my lips. Men are such bores
men are such bores men are such bores they take so long to
realise anything. One could create the world while waiting for
them to connect an apparently disparate idea. Men are such
bores. Someone just had to say her name and my cock stiffened.
She would glance at me across the room—a split second—and
she would fuck me in that moment. And she would know. I had
made mistakes with all of them. I was too young to know any different with Ursula, too lost to know any different with
Holfy . . . I don't know . . . too stupid to know Holfy was the

one. The good thing. I write to Holfy with my address. Then I write another letter and include some of the bits I wrote in her darkroom.

Doors I had closed are flung open. Terror flies at me, yellow bats in the darkness, surprised by light. All my fears flap about, winged with a thousand cruelties. Desire runs through me faster than blood. I sit up in the bed sweating with the fierceness of a dream still racing through me. I imagine Holfy sleeping on her stomach, her hands tucked under her chest. The memory of her dispelling the nightmare. Her cunt tastes like butter melting on hot toast. When I am in her she squelches with joy. The sound of her lovemaking entrances me like the first time I heard corn crackling in its leaves in a July sun. She walks differently. When she moves, her legs are alive with knowing that I have been between them and will be between them again and again. I get dressed and go out and drive through the darkness. Every night sleep fails and I go out and drive the dirt roads as if it's a job. How strange these back roads are, straight as book edges and cutting across each other like the grid of Manhattan but unpeopled. It is as if they are some grand abandoned scheme.

I am barricaded inside myself, a crazed bird on the floor of its cage, exhausted. I am driving off Howth Head. Ursula Ursula Ursula Ursula. There is no consolation in today's wisdom over yesterday's folly. I know too much now. I failed her and there is nothing. I watch the needle climb to one hundred. The car begins to dip and hurtle towards the sea of corn. Anything to force the sadness away. There is nothing at all happening

between us, only the widening of the years. I wake in the bed
before the car crashes. I lie down to sleep and in sleep move close
to Holfy, smelling her hair, scent of oranges from her shampoo.
What am I doing? What am I doing with this child of a woman?
I wake and sleep and wake and the days pass and in the
peopleless fields I lose sense of time, am no longer sure when
I wake up if the dream of driving through the darkness was
a dream or if I did get up in the night and am back in bed and
waking.

I drive out onto the highway looking for a town. It's impossible
to tell from the highway signs what will be a town and what will
be nothing. Everything is marked with the same democratic
sense of importance. Next exit, wherever it is.

It turns out to be another nowhere. I stop at the first bar on
Main Street. All these Midwestern bars are the same, only the
hopeless inhabit them. I have stopped drinking. It wasn't the
drink I needed, it was the sight of humanity. A television in the
corner. It's so long since I have seen one that it has the appearance of a box of magical puppets. I stare at it with incomprehen-
sion. My eyes focus on its world. A woman in a smart suit talking
into a chunky microphone; some kind of disaster behind her.
Her voice, her gestures are inexorably ineluctable. I look down at
my root beer and grin at the sound of Ursula quoting *inex-
orablyineluctable* as fast as she can, mocking constipated poet-
words, words stuck on a page to say what does not need to be
said, words to make up feelings that you never truly felt. The
newswoman must have a number of tones, of looks that present

all our tragedies, our follies. A man is standing talking with her. He too is a presenter of news. There is more subtlety in her plucked face. I walk out into the sunlight. Even this nowhere is too much for me. I go back to Lone Tree with its 401 inhabitants. I go back to the barn, to my wisdom. My nerves are much better. There is the tiniest pink hue in the sky, as if creation is approaching pleasure.

I have been running a long time and now I can run no further. The sky spreads out endless blue, denying God. I need a God today. I need someone to shake. I see myself putting a gun in my mouth. Baird put the shotgun against his chest and missed the heart the first time. The police car parked two hundred yards away, waiting, deciding how to approach. He discharged the cartridge and shot himself again. That ended it.

> It was not days nor weeks nor months you were leaving—years you were leaving me. What I sensed, feared, for so long, was always happening. I had felt battered by your betrayal (I should say betrayals but there is only ever one) and disgusted by my innocence for so long that I had lost sight of myself. It seems extraordinary I stayed awake nights blaming myself; I fought so hard to keep you. I see the words shaping on your lips—when did I battle to hold on to it all, yes? You could never see it. You would not count the years of listening as loving. Listening to the great silence from you. Taking you in my mouth (yes, I never did like that and I shouldn't have lied when you asked). So much I did in understanding you. Planting flowers. None of this was ever apparent to you. You would have expected it and not gloried in how much I cared for you. I had said words I thought I would say to

no man. Do you know what was the worst moment? How
sad it is to be so certain you have no idea. Certainty is a
kind of death. You had the gall to look at me expecting a
reconciliation after being inside another woman; it meant
as little as that; you did not see it the way I did: when you
were inside me, you were touching my soul—even the
times I did not enjoy it, we were touching souls. Even
now, although I care nothing for you, I feel like vomiting
at the memory you were inside a woman and then came
to me and put that part of you in me. How would you
have felt if I had done that? It makes me sick to think that
you may not have minded at all, that love does not hold
such sacredness for you. I thought it was the end of me. It
wasn't. It was the beginning. After the steel chill of
parting I feel what I had not even begun to consider—I
feel freedom.

I drop the letter on the deck. The citronella bucket seems to
attract as many mosquitoes as it keeps away. I light another cigarette. I touch the letter off the flame of the matchstick. I go down
to the car and turn it on, blast the air conditioner way up. I turn
right and head for the highway. The cassette player is broken; I
turn on the radio. The world is still there, talking on the radio.
The same eager and self-important American voices on each
station. I come across a news channel: an explosion somewhere. Dreadful solemnity scarcely containing itself. I am sick of
it all. It never changes. I switch channels . . . *and with the support
of listeners like you . . .* I switch the radio off and listen to the air-
conditioning. I turn onto a back road, dirt billowing into the sky.
Fear twists in me; the fear that is always there in the gut. I stop
the car and get out. My spectacles steam with the heat. I walk for

a long time, pass a man with a dog. Two turtles hanging from each hand. Gun under his arm.

—Evenin', he says.

I return his wary smile. Cornfields stretching for miles. Nothing but the eerie clatter of stalks, dry with the cruel August heat. They must be eight feet tall. Row after row of well-behaved corn. It stops with purposeful abruptness. It has the same effect that coming up out of the subway on Fourteenth and Eighth always has on me; space and light. The cornfields become hogfields. Dozens of little A-frames. The hogs themselves are nowhere to be seen. At the edge of the field stands a man in a long robe, arms out, fingers spread: beseeching. He looks, for all the world, like an apparition. I look around. I expect to hear a snigger. It's ridiculous to be frightened. I can hear for miles off. I walk closer. A statue. A stone plaque, a foot or so to its left:

JEAN BROUSSARD
A burgher of Calais
Auguste Rodin 1840–1917

I look around again. It makes no sense. A sudden breeze and the gentle rough clack of the corn leaves. Even the breeze carries suspicions. But there is no one to explain. There is no one to listen to questions. Only the sky, the cornfields, and the incongruous statue. I laugh at the stupidity of myself; there is nothing: nothing but a pile of broken images from a past littered with petty dishonesties; nothing left but a tangle of misunderstandings. I turn and run. I run and run, the corn leaves lashing my face, whipping with the fierceness of Holfy's belt, the night my father lashed me for wetting the bed, lashing me in the face with the belt. Ruth screaming. I am running and running, the insanity of running frightening me, forcing me to run faster, to blot out the madness, to run as if I had purpose, and laughing and wet with sweat. Blood is running out of my nose into my mouth and I'm lying on the ground with the taste of blood and dirt in my mouth with the sky over me and I get up from the dizzy blueness and run again. I stumble, fall, pick myself up. Cornstalks whip and creak. I fall, my side sore with exertion. No sound but the sound of my breathing and my heartbeat. The sky is cloudlessly blue, makes me long for the greyness of Dublin. But Dublin is too long ago. Ursula is too long ago; my father loading the car with Ruth's things; my hand lifting the bottle of Jeyes fluid to my lips as a dare with Ruth; the blink of time that was Holfy eating my kisses. There is no space for forgiveness. The corn clatters off itself in rebuke.

The earth, hot and sun-cracked. Alone with no one but myself. *You don't have a self.* Holfy lied about her age. All this *activity* for a me that isn't. A bird steps out in front of me. A pheasant. It could be a Martian for all the difference it makes. It stands stock-still, staring into the stalks, has the appearance of some bizarre mirage shimmering in the humidity. Tear tracks burn into my skin. Bronzed feathers. Mottled with black and green. Road-runner. *Mee Mee.* Its eye, deep in a fleshy red patch, swivels, takes me in, swivels back, and in two graceless strides it flaps into the sky, the breeze of its whirring wings convincing me of its presence, and is gone. *Kok-cack, kok-kack,* it screeches into the silence it leaves behind. There is a room that is empty of everything except regret. I will die some day and Ursula will not have walked in it. She will stand by my grave and think nothing happened: believe I did not know this place.

A thin white trail scratches the blue sky. The plane is so high it's scarcely visible. Coming from somewhere far away, and going somewhere far away. Must make Midwesterners feel the insignificance of life here, of life happening elsewhere. The white line carves through the sky, bisects me. I am looking into myself. The end of the line fades. I was wrong about Agnes Martin. It's everything stripped. It's the opposite of ego. It's finding the thing. I understand nothing. Life is fundamental accuracy of statement—not art. *Life* is. Then—only then—art. Martin *was* religion—that's why she didn't believe in it. One day the heart stops.

A child found me in the field. They were detasseling the corn. Three weeks pass in the hospital. I remember a man I don't recognise come visit and I remember listening to him say the burns from the sun will heal and I will pull through. His name is Parizeh.

Two fat packets are waiting in the mailbox when I get out of hospital, both from New York. Depression is never darkness. Darkness is relief. Sleep is relief. Depression is the brightness of a sunny day, flowers fat in their blooming, two people greeting each other on the street and laughing. Depression is beautiful music that does nothing to the emotions. Depression is seeing this and knowing it doesn't matter. Nothing matters. If there was someone to phone I would but there isn't.

I am left looking at myself. I have always been unhappy. I look up at the sun and doze. The evening sun is as close as I get to content. Cars pass by on the highway in the distance. This is my life. It was my birthday today. Birthdays were such fun as a child. Playing with a Lego set. Red and green and white and blue. Where does life go? Where do the smiles go? Does someone else smile the smiles I've stopped smiling? I open the packets. A postcard spills out. Six words: *You imitate Durrell badly. Forget Durrell.*

Then a PS: *Still like you.*

Life gathers in such phrases.

She's written her comments on the back of my writing.

Let me put it another way: writing is like painting. You do it. Keep doing it. Feel it working through the brush. Writers have the advantage of never running the risk of going too far. There's always the last draft. The stress in painting is one stroke too many. Why I turned to photography. Photography is definable. No matter how many clicks there are, they are all finite. Then the magic of the darkroom. Processing is Christmas presents.

I came across this today: That for which we find words is something dead in our hearts. There is always a kind of contempt in the act of speaking. Nietzsche.

The first time I heard a woodpecker. He was inside a small trunk that was no fatter than a wrist. I climbed over the small fence and listened. Like a timid but insistent child he was, tapping. I tapped back and he stopped. Then tap tap tap. All the genius of creation stored in such a small and simple bird. There was a time I thought I would do anything for love. Thought that it was possible. That there would be a divine coupling. Someone who would see the world as I see the world. Such an atrocious assumption. I've kept the old rotary phone and got it hooked up yesterday. I sat there looking at it like it was the enemy for half an hour. Haven't called anyone yet. The options they give: I didn't know what half of them were, call waiting, call blocking, Jesus, she went on and on and all I knew is I didn't want any of them. You have to pay to have people leave you alone.

The presents I bought my mother as a child. Dishcloths, delft, cutlery. Perfume with all the subtlety of disinfectant. Earrings that looked like toys hanging from her ears. Rigor mortis is setting into the tulips. Brilliance happens by accident. One day, sitting there and it happens. The woodpecker deep in the bowl of a tree. Pecking. Staring at it and listening and its mate lands on a branch and sings a warning and out it flies, a fluttering flash of feathers gone and nothing but silence left.

One day Holfy was not there and I wanted her to be. I was angry at her for forgetting but as I sat there and as I waited and waited for her something in me closed. It is unnameable whatever it is that closed. I danced that night in the apartment. For the first time in my life I danced on my own.

I felt the cold edge on our love when I didn't run out after her in the morning when I knew she had forgotten to take the film out of the fridge, I felt it in the note I didn't leave tucked in her bag to wish her luck on the job that morning in the Puck Building. I felt the coldness in the things I didn't do for her, in the things that she had no idea I wanted to do for her. Love became not doing but loving her still. The curious thing is that she didn't notice and then I learned something: people don't miss what they don't want.

Mr. Parizeh comes to visit with his son. He asks if I'd be interested in a couple of pups he needs rid of, looks out the window towards his truck away from any hint of kindness. I walk out to the truck and look in at the pups scurrying around the back of the truck, two sets of paws up on the tailgate. I lift them out and set them on the dirt. They run about yelping with happiness.

I go to the supermarket every day. I walk around the store the same way: carrots, potatoes, milk and butter at the end of the aisle, meat, bread, beer if it's a Friday. Not that Friday exists in America. There are no patterns except the patterns we make. I fool myself into thinking I'm in Dublin sometimes. I have stopped exchanging the currency rate in my mind. I think in dollars. I am no longer surprised at how expensive it is to buy a deliciously red and tasteless tomato. I have learned to live in America through its supermarkets. No one told me what the stores were: Wal-Mart, Econofoods, Quiktrip, Sam's. There was no identity in their names. Their identity reveals itself through the people who shop in these stores. Even before I go inside I can tell by the cars in the lot who will be there and what they will be buying to create their dream futures, making worlds that will never exist. Paper or plastic, they say at the checkout. Do you want a paper or plastic sack to take your dreams home. Life is about finding ways to control. Shopping is control. I am a consumer now and I love it. It is as reassuring as a cigarette. It tells me who I am. This, more than anything, is what I need.

It happens slowly. One day you hear a name yelled on a street, called out in a film, the eye catches sight of it on an envelope in some office, and it causes no pain. There is nothing but a memory, faded like the sounds of childhood. There is nothing left. Her name is drained of meaning. At first, I thought it meant an emptiness akin to death, but I was wrong. The emptiness is something precious. It is the wisdom of finally knowing myself. The layer of need under it. Most men have it, a wordless, unadmitted need. I must sound cynical. I am, a little. For a long time I thought something was wrong with me. I wanted a woman that—I laugh at my stupidity—would be everything I wanted in a woman. How utterly ridiculous an idea I had. I couldn't get a word processor that would do everything I wanted—how could I ever get it from a woman. How little good it does the soul.

I go about my business, smile at people, keep myself tidy, go to bed at the same hour, get up at the same hour. I maintain a surface of normality. I tell the pups we are normal when I feed them and they wag their tails. I have wasted so many years. The pups bark. They want to go out. Go out, I say, opening the door. They shoulder each other and rush through the door out into the forest as if the day will bring them something that it did not bring them yesterday. Pearl jostles Boogie and she barks viciously, and they go their separate ways. They stop and sniff the air, waiting. Then they run back to the screen door I have already closed. They sit and wait at it. The same tedious routine every morning. Every morning I wake up and know Ruth is dead. The loss of her grows every day. Him too. Life is tiring, just with trying not to hate the past for being here. I hang soap bars on the trees to stop the deer eating the leaves.

I go for days without talking. I don't shoo the dogs out of the way. I am learning my place in the world. At night there are the cicadas. They deafen the night with their mating calls. There is an owl somewhere and her hoot is calming. The only sound in the house is the electric drone of the fridge coming on and off. Sometimes, when the silence builds, when it becomes loaded like a gun, I cough and the cough is enough to dispel the loneliness. It is a strange loneliness that has soaked into me because I am not lonely for people. For a long time I thought it was loneliness for Ruth and my life with Ursula. But that is not true. I am lonely for myself. I have gone away a long time ago and I have only just noticed. I have deserted myself.

I read in the paper that a fourteen-year-old swam out into Hoover Lake and tempted a swan out of the reeds with muffins. Then he beheaded the swan. The swan's mate has not moved for six days. She stays by the murder spot.

The cicadas are screeching greedily in the night. I get so drunk I wet my trousers. I lift the telephone and listen to the tone. Vulgar hum. I list everyone I know. Imagine a conversation with them. Talking on it with Holfy. With deaddeaddaddy. With deaddeadRuth. With Ursula. With the fuck of a mother I once had. That time when the balloon burst and she lifted me off the counter and hugged me. There is no number to dial. Can't think of a single person I can talk to without apology or disgust swallowing my words.

Everything is nonsense. It is the greatest nonsense of all believing

I had to be alone, that I enjoyed the solitude. The phone rings one day and my heart races. I don't care who it is, I am happy to hear a sound not of my own making. Then it stops before I pick it up.

Who knows what is true, what is accurate. It seems I have never been happy but I must have been. Is it that my mind is drawn only to the saddest moments? My parents arguing in the hall and asking us to decide which one we wanted to go with. The abject terror I felt. Where were we going to go? It was night-time. We couldn't go out in the bad night. We would disappear if we left the flat and went out into the night. I looked up at my mother and father and at Ruth. Who would pick who? I picked Franko, the man who used to come into the shop every night, because I couldn't decide between them. I don't know how it got resolved in the end. All I remember is that fear that I would not be with my parents. I don't remember thinking about not seeing my sister again. Just the terror of the cold, black night and not seeing one or the other of my parents again. I don't remember if I had school the next day. I remember I had a coat on and I remember staring up at the door handle of the flat and wanting to reach up to it and have us all go in and go to bed.

The balloon. I was sitting on the counter watching everyone come in and out and buy their sweets and books. I was watching my mother and father take back the books and thumb through them rapidly with their fingers. The edge of their thumbs would tell them if a page was missing. Sitting up on the counter I could see how exciting the world was. You had to be as tall as a grown-up to understand what was going on. Up on the counter I could see and understand everything. It was coming up to Christmas and I had a blue balloon in my hands. Sometimes I would rub my finger on its squelchy belly and my mother would tell me to stop. A man came in and bought a couple of books. He was smoking a dirty cigarette. He looked as wise as God must look, and as if he must know everything there was to know. He bought chocolate and packed up his books. Then he held the cigarette to the blue balloon and there was a bang and the air snapped in my face. It was like a bad miracle. This is all I remember. Sometimes I think I remember the wrong things. I remember the plastic curtains that separated our shop from the flat we lived in. They were black and yellow and red strips of plastic that swooshed back and forth all day long and whichever side of them I was on I always imagined there was a magic cave on the other side that was full of riches and deep mysteries.

I would discover the pleasure and the laughter of being with a woman. There would be books and films and washing dishes and taking clothes to the launderette and our jobs to pay the rent but they would be the things we had to do until next we could be in bed together. This was the only reality. Nothing mattered more than the pleasure of our nakedness and the simple happiness of our warm bodies that surprised us with unceasing pleasures.

There is a hypnotic sense in this, as if I am leading towards some greater understanding, as if there is some inevitable truth that will reveal itself. There is not. Except perhaps the danger of nostalgia. Because it didn't last with Ursula. We had six years together. An awful lot of time to arrive at nothing but a nut of bitterness and guilt. It is the insipid and insidious edge of niceness that cut into the truth and buried a lie. I did not want to complain about the sex with her. So I lied, and so did she. But desire ran inside me and flooded me in bed with her every night and I prayed for the desire to go away but it didn't. I tried not to touch her. I tried not to bother her and slowly, when I began to realise that it was not getting better, that she might never get better, that I might not get better, I began to hate my desire. And the hours passed, and the days, and the weeks, and the months, and the years, and still nothing was different. I no longer blamed the desire. I blamed her.

Turn thoughts off. Turn them off. They're no use. It's done. That's all there is to it. The drink is taking hold of me. I'm thirsty for it even as I drink it. I want to send my little Ursula a post-card, tell her everything. But no. The other way. Walk away. Get up and work on the barn, even with the heat. Work the only solace.

Lightning in the bright summer evening. It starts to thunder a little before nine and it goes on into the early morning. The electricity goes off. The sudden crash of wind lashing through trees in darkness. I stay up all night watching the earth showing itself its splendour. The sound of wood ripping, lightning strobes flashing on the fields. Rain. Rain so heavy I turn the radio off and listen to its thunderous assault. Loneliness gnaws at the dead-ness in me. It wrings my guts with a plea for company. Ursula. Holfy. Anyone. I could talk to anyone. The sky flashes, threaten-ing me.

◇ ◇ ◇

The end of marriage was a quiet, tree-lined street, waiting for spring. Trees are courageous without leaves. We were going about our lives talking intensely about everything except the end of it all. And then one night I say it as we are driving home from that movie.

Stopped at that light in Blackrock, talking about her article. I look up at the large Santa Claus over the shopping centre and say I love you and you love me but it's over and I don't want it to be so but it is the truth and the light turns green and she says yes it is true and we drive home. It was tiny lies that lodged between us. Bindweed tightening around a tree. I am drinking a bottle of vodka a day now.

Winter comes bitterly. I go to the local flower shop to buy a potted green plant to celebrate. When the florist hears my Irish accents she perks up.

—It closes up at night, says the woman, joining her hands.

She smiles at my disbelief.

—It's a prayer plant. That's its name.

Then she mentions the Irish wedding and I make the mistake of feigning interest. When she invites me she sees my reluctance.

—I divorced two years ago. Being a florist makes a girl realistic. I've sold a lot of wedding bouquets in those two years and I'm sure glad none of them were mine. Name's Moira.

She sticks her hand out just as a hefty woman comes into the shop, wide with a sweaty smile.

—Morning, Justine.

—I'll phone you Moira the Realist.

I take her business card off the counter. Justine smiles at me, oozing suspicion.

—Whatever.

—Thanks for the prayer plant.

—You betcha.

She is already chatting with Obesity.

There's an oil spill on the highway and the traffic is backed up for fifteen miles. We sit there, stuck in her pickup. Elijah is skating around in the back, barking. We are already too late for the church so we go straight to the hotel. White crooked letters on a blackboard spell O'Hara and Flaherty reception. Queuing at the buffet, a man nudges in front of me. I am shocked by his rudeness in this country where staying in line is a commandment. I turn, see he is a priest and am about to say something when he smiles at me and says in a thick Irish accent:

—Grand spread, isn't it? And as grand a couple as ever I've married.

—You must be starving with the hunger.

He claps me on the shoulder, winks, the secret knowingness of the fickle Irish in America, playing it up for all its worth.

—Begob, he says, another Irishman. Nothing like a wedding Mass to put a hunger on you.

He nods and spoons meat onto his plate and looks at me again, long smile.

—Are you long over?

—Long enough.

—What's the news from home?

How he says the word *home.* The faded rosiness of a place that no longer exists. I imagine that he is ten, perhaps fifteen years out of Ireland. Frank Patterson Irish leg-opener voice. Begob and musha and arra how are you.

—Brutal.

—But the North, he says, isn't that on the mend?

—Yes, the church are staying out of it. It helps.

—You're an awful man.

Impossible to insult him. He claps me on the shoulder again.

—Is there no roast beef here at all? he asks the server on the other side of the steaming silver pans. He's wearing a grey wig with a hairline at the back that could have been cut with a garden shears.

We go to the Ace of Spades out by the lake, a lake made to enhance the nightclub's appeal. Hardly needed. A lot, the size of a football pitch, is full of cars. We park and cut through the maze, pass a car shaking gently and pretend not to see it. The club is huge—as big as the Pontoon Ballroom my father painted in Mayo. A couple are dancing on the floor with theatrical precision. Euphoria in the middle of blue-collar nowhereness. The dancer's hand slides up and down her body in tortured ecstasy. She runs her hands between her nyloned thighs.

—Choreographed sex.

—Know them?

Moira wrinkles her nose. The couple swirl, the woman mouthing the words of the song. Her mouth is losing its passion and her eyes close. I stop smiling at their spectacle. She is dancing with the man she had hoped her husband might be, the man she dreamed she married. I feel pity for his Travolta-like grimaces. A

crowd comes in, noisy with its own excitement. The floor begins
to swallow up the couple. I have no idea what I am doing here
with this flower woman.

—Dance? You Irish still dance?

—Sure.

It's all seventies music, Abba and the like. A slow set comes on.
The skin on her palms is rough like a kitchen scourer. We are
uncomfortable so close to each other, smile, go and get a drink at
the bar. She tells me she needs some work done on the apartment
she's bought. It went for a dime. She asks if I know of a handyman. No, but I know the song. Moira breeds rabbits.

Surface is everything. I watch the sky. A hawk waits in the
breeze. His wings are still, like a kite. Light plays with the leaves
of the tree. He drops like a stone and just as quickly takes off
with a prone creature in his claws. The land is exhausted here.
Dust rises for miles. Years wasted. Regret is useless but it snaps at
my ankle like a dog afraid of itself. A hundred years from now,
what difference any of it. I go in and make tea, such as it can be,
in this city of poisoned water. It takes a long time to see.

Moira and I are talking in bed, she's listening to me talking and
I'm happy to be talking even if it's the worn-out past. It's someone
listening.

I stopped saying Da at school. The boys used to go Daaaa and
call me Sheepshite. Then they called me Shovelhead because of
the shape of my face. I stopped lots of things in school. I stopped

talking in school. I stopped talking and I listened and waited for
it to be over. It would get better when I got into secondary
school. It got worse. I was twelve years old. I told Daddy I was
leaving after the intermediate exams. He told me I was not leaving until after my leaving certificate exams and that was all there
was to it. I was told I was going to get a good job. I waited. For
five years I sat in class trying not to look at the clock. For five
years the clock crawled to five minutes to four and the bell rang
and I waited for the teacher to tell me it was alright to pack my
schoolbag. And one day I was seventeen and childhood was over
and my father said now go out and get a job and I did—I went to
work. I was seeing Ursula. I was a man. I went and sprayed tele-
visions in Clastronix. That was the good job. I began to fall in
love with paint. I began to watch closely. I watched the arc of
paint fanning across the sheets of metal. I watched the others and
tried to see who had talent and who didn't. Gerry had it. Slowly,
I began to realise the mistakes I made were not simply in the
wrist. Mistakes came out of the crook of the elbow, and up
through the soles of the feet, the bend of the knee, the blink of
the eye. Mistakes came out of the whole body. Slowly, I understood my eye had little to do with it. Paint shot out of the gun
too quickly for the eye to right wrongs. I began to relax more,
and as the weeks passed, the muscle in my arm strengthened, my
wrist ached less at the end of the day and my neck was not as
sore when I woke in the dark winter mornings. Now, when I
painted, I started to close my eyes, and I could feel the paint hit
the sheet of dull plastic. I began to listen to the hiss of paint as it
flew across the sheet, began to follow the rhythm of paint. I
would fall into a trance and then, one morning, I heard the paint

sing, paint delighting in its own beauty. When I had decided that
I had it mastered completely, when I believed I could paint without concentration, I examined my work, and to my horror, discovered it flawed. Paint could never be mastered.

—You make factory work sound real poetic.

—Everything is poetry to the young idealist.

Every morning, as I changed into my work clothes and put on
my gloves and mask, I would listen in a stupor to the crude talk
on the floor. I pretended not to be interested. I probably even
convinced myself that I was not listening, but I was rapt. Beyond
the facade of silence and disgust, I loved it all. I discovered the
beauty of paint. We all went out every night and got drunk and
we all hated the work and we all loved being grown-up. No one
called me Shovelhead anymore.

I was in love with Ursula. We married and I wanted a better
job to show her I was better than anything she thought I was. We
moved out of Dorset Street and into the place in Harcourt
Street. We had parties in there all the time. I didn't invite the
people from the factory, not even Gerry. People from the *Tribune*
came and got drunk. And they all tore strips off whoever the
government was and were ferocious about the way the underprivileged were treated. It was the first time I heard people using
the word underprivileged who weren't talking on the radio or
the television. I loved those parties. Mixing with the best of
them. Loved hearing them talk shit about the working class, a
class they themselves despised outside of the words coming
out of their well-fed mouths. The most disconcerting moment
about moving up the class ladder is realising your people are
a pawn. I was *of* the working class unlike these masticating

morons who were *for* it. I stop talking, turn to Moira and see she
is asleep.

Winter passes slowly, then without much of a spring, summer
erupts. I am painting the hall door a glistening black. NPR has a
day dedicated to war: a debate about gun control. The usual banter. The sun crackles on the paintbrush. Moira drives by and
stops and yells out the window that black's a bad colour, attracts
the heat, then drives off, laughing. The door shines with the
importance of its new coat. I make a vodka gimlet and sit and
admire it. The paint dries in minutes. Ireland is mentioned on the
radio. I reach down and turn it up. *Peace: now what?* says an American voice, serious as granite. *A look at a people emerging from decades
of hate.* Voices speak. Lap over each other. Irish voices. Snippets
of opinions. Tired, angry words pop like surprised bubbles. I
make another drink and sit back, happy to hate the autistic pit of
the North. The sun is beginning to drop, still brash with heat.
Ireland. Fuck them, let them kill each other.

I open my eyes to Ursula's voice ringing in my ears. Sweat
running down my spectacles. Her voice is speaking to me. I look
around, terrified. Her voice is sharp as sunshine.

—I don't believe that. It's complete nonsense, she says.

I close my eyes and press my fingers against my lids.

—I don't believe that was ever true about women. I don't believe
you are taking anything seriously in asking that question—

—But surely the very concept of beauty has been with us since
the beginning of time?

Dead air.

—Has it not?

I stare at the radio, waiting for her answer.

—Not as long as stupidity, she says.

I fell in love with you many times, Ursula. The seductiveness of that voice. I laugh out loud at the fight in you.

I go into the city to buy some Christmas presents. Disgusted as I am by it, nostalgia gnaws at me. I buy the *Tribune* to ease the homesickness. It's full of colour advertisements and friendly, fluffy articles. Large photographs of skinny models. I trudge through the heavy snow-laden streets and find a seat by the window in the Tobacco Bowl. I read an article about the decline of the microwave; one about Northern Ireland; I read what's on television—Ireland shrunk into the TV page. A boxed review of a programme about abortion; the reviewer's initials in the bottom corner: UF. I look up from the newspaper and East Washington Street shocks me with its presence; two snowplows scooping up hills of snow like ducks dredging through mucky puddles for food. People pass, hidden in clothes to fight the freezing weather. We can acclimatise to anything. I see Ursula's face, flushed with the cold, in front of me, feel her slide next to me in the booth and hug my arm with her being. The smell of her perfume. There is no ending, she goes on forever. Reading her, even such a frugal snippet, is like being inside her. I can see her sitting at the kitchen table with the electric fire on, scribbling agitated notes. To know her so well and to have wasted it all. I hate all the days and nights I gave her. Hate all the fights we had trying to resolve everything. Hate all the times I apologised to her. Hate that I loved her once more dearly than anything or anyone in this world and that time is past.

Months pass. I walk for hours on the dirt roads that separate
the cornfields. My mother's breath on my face. The smell of lager
off her, the excitement at the anticipation of her coming into me
at night, kissing me and frightening me with her large eyes. A
horse neighing somewhere. A dog barks back at it and then I see
the house. It is in bad repair; the kind of house one expects an
outlaw to be holing up in, waiting for the final showdown. There
are three unkempt horses; one of them, the white one, large with
foal. It takes me a long while to realise she is looking at me. Her
stillness unnerves me. She is holding a paintbrush in her hand
and she looks as if she is about to fire it like a knife thrower in a
circus. I clear my throat. *I heard your horses.* My voice floats across
the back of the grey pony. The fear in the air is mine; she is
unafraid. I want her to know that I am friendly but the notion of
my friendliness is probably absurd to her. I look around, expecting to see Holfy hiding somewhere. It's too perfect: a woman
painting in the middle of a cornfield. It must be a joke. She has
the same build as Holfy and she is about sixty feet from me. I
cough in warning as I approach her. She is older than she seemed
from afar, strength in her eyes: a clarity. When she looks at me I
can see she is not simply looking at me, she is looking at what I
am. A lit cigarette between her fingers seems forgotten. The dog
by her side watches me with the same mute lack of interest. She
lifts her hand indifferently and takes a drag out of it. It is of no
account to her who I am. She absorbs the air around me. Her
eyes are unnervingly calm. Something else, too, but I can only
sense it. The light perhaps. The sky falling off into blueness
behind the shack. Old attachments. They pull inside and push
me towards her. I am an abstraction to her. A shade falling beside

a patch of sunlight; a splash of colour in her painting. My
mother's face on those drunken Saturday nights. The smell off
her breath when she kissed me goodnight. The way she is holding the paintbrush. As if it is part of her. The ease she has with it
as if the paint is coming out of her and not the brush. The rigid
ease of her hand at work. The longer I look at her the more
insane she appears. An old woman living here, alone, unafraid.
As if to correct me I hear a clang, like the carriage of a train
shouldering itself into silence. A youth is straightening a gas
cylinder against the side of the house. He is blond, strong,
unmistakably American. He runs a chain through the ugly tor-
pedo shapes and locks them without once looking over. I lift my
hand and start a wave. She watches me, waiting for me to go. I
start off down the road, whistling. His appearance highlights her
foreignness. Something about her is un-American. She is dark,
Hispanic perhaps. The air is charged with my strained noncha-
lance. He is probably still not looking at me. He is no more than
fifteen years old and yet there is a rude violence about his cool-
ness. Of course she could not get by utterly alone; the heating
would have to be brought in for her.

I am a mile or so from the house. I wonder about passing it today.
She might shoot this time. America is trigger happy, and here in
the Midwest the lock-and-load neurosis roars though silent fields,
the perceptible sound of gunfire itself. I walk on; stop. I don't
want her to know I am curious. I am no threat, too slight to be a
danger, even the kid could take me on. She is feeding the horses.
She puts her bucket down and walks to the gate.

—What do you want?

Her question is so direct, the flatness of a worn stone on a beach. Stillness at the centre of her stare. Ruth skimming stones, three bounces, four bounces. Once, she skimmed eleven bounces. Our world record. Sacredness is unaware of itself. The woman turns away from me. She is not impatient for an answer, she is uninterested.

—I don't want anything.

My voice is unexpectedly indignant. It shivers in the cold air. She pauses with her back still to me; nods her head as if that is explanation enough, walks slowly back to the munching horses. *To say hello,* I shout across the field. My voice waivers between friendliness and irritation. But already she is absorbed in her work. I think about stepping over the low rusted fence. Confronting her. But she has done nothing except ignore a busybody. I walk for about an hour, feel their presence behind me but know it's my imagination. I turn back.

As I pass her house I think of some ruse for approaching the door, a question of some sort if the boy is in. But there is a blind look to the house that warns me off. I meet her a mile down the road. She is walking with the dog. She beckons for me to follow her.

—I wanted a home here. I like the bleakness. It leaves the mind open. This place was for sale. No one wanted to buy it. Like your place. The farmer shot his wife and his daughter-in-law in the kitchen.

—This is the Baird farm? I thought it was on the other side of the highway.

—This is it. They were chopping potatoes: the wife's belly and the bones from her back hit the wall. I hang Frida Kahlo there. Big joke. No one wants to buy a place where death is. They left the pig houses, they left everything. The murdered farm, I call this place. People say it's morbid. They spend their lives dead and they say morbid.

The door opens from the only other room. The boy comes out, the corner of a wardrobe visible behind him. She sees my mind working. She smiles at the shock I'm trying to hide.

—Why did he kill them?

—Ronald Reagan. The banks shut farms.

—It was for sale that long?

—People are afraid.

—Of what?

—Who needs a *what*? My name is Toscana.

I lie in bed thinking of the old woman lying in her bed. The boy must have parents. The noise of the fan keeps me awake so I get up and go into the kitchen. I pick up a plum and squeeze it for freshness. Juice breaks through the skin. Ursula would write a sensuous poem about such a plum. I hate knowing that I hate being alone. Holfy doesn't answer my letters. No matter. I get up and make coffee. Toscana is just some crazy woman but at least she's content in her madness. I can't bear this middle of nothing-ness any longer, can't bear the idea of another winter, this living without purpose. I finish the coffee and go to the Hawkeye and buy a ticket for New York. Moira agrees to take Pearl and Boogie but she will not be held responsible if Elijah eats them. She'll see to the sale of the barn if it ever sells she says. Great at telling it as it is are Midwesterners.

Manhattan is frozen with heat. Not even memories are left in New York. Life moves too quickly there to let memories gather anywhere. Street signs still the same: Jane, Horatio, Little West Twelfth, Bethune, Perry, Ninth Avenue. Pearl, Fulton, Canal, Elizabeth. Lafayette, Dominick, Cornelia, Bedford, Commerce, Barrow. Gansevoort. Restaurants with their cluttered greedy tables. Small bricks that give the buildings their quaintness. Turn a corner off Seventh Avenue and find a quiet step to eat one of those Middle Eastern take-away thingys. And it's early morning and sleepy workers hose clean the sidewalks all over the tired and dirty city. A Mexican sitting on the corner by the flower shop. His shirt. Welcome to America. Now Speak English.

Gone with the rush of the subway. I thought there was some sense to the way I was living, something unique about it all and that one day I would be rewarded and my choices—even the callous ones—would make sense. There is nothing left now except the bad decisions and the indistinct path of words leading the way to a semblance of integrity.

The meat shop is gone on Gansevoort Street, magically converted to an architect's office. I peer in through the shutters. The old hoarding that advertised the butcher's wares hangs inside the new trendy office, a hip relic of the past. Someone will pay money for it one day. I go to Florent for coffee to steel myself. But Florent is closed. I walk to the Serivalli playground on the corner of Thirteenth. The sound of a car passing on Eighth

Avenue. Even the Empire, lit with red and green, seems deserted.
I go back. I have to face her.

I ring the bell and wait. His name still on the door. Robert
Tansey. RIP Robert Tansey. A garbage bag moves in the doorway
and I leap back looking for a rat. A hand touches my knee and a
frail voice asks for change. I stare down at the darkness. The
smallest I have is a ten. Have a good day, says the voice. Music
from the top of the stairs. I decide to use the key. A black man,
immaculately dressed in a black suit, meets me at the top of the
stairs. The hallway has a new smell. Ray Charles singing with that
smile of his.

—How can I help you?

—*You* can't.

—You rang *my* bell.

I stop on the stairwell and look at the man and point past him
at the open door.

—I rang that bell.

—Right. You rang my bell.

I try to look beyond him into the apartment.

—How did you get in here, Sir?

I hold up the key, a black man and a white man facing each
other. America's defeat.

—You have a key to my apartment?

His blackness soaks into me. He appraises me a second longer.

—Just a minute, Sir.

He closes the door quietly. Suddenly her absence is apparent.
She is gone. The apartment as it was flashes through my mind,
the bed up against the window, the scattered books, the night I
awoke to her watching the video of her wedding, the first time I

was making tea and reaching for the blue jug with sugar in it. I run down the stairs and out into the street, I run until I am breathless at Thirteenth Street.

I think of Kahlo dying on the veterinary table and my crack afterwards about the N word and wonder if she rented it to the black as a last joke. Gerry might know where she is. I phone from the street. No answer there. No one will be around. Bill. Bill might be in town. Bingo. Bingo Bill. I ring information to find somewhere to rent a car. It takes twenty minutes in this 24/7 city to find somewhere that can rent me a car. I have to take the train from Grand Central to White Plains.

People want to help, that is part of the problem. We are insane, all of us. I feel insanity flowing through my veins, the insanity of being human. The painter living in the Baird house. That was what she was and happy in it. She needs nothing from the world, the purest form of madness. Then there are those on the periphery of it, those who sit and drink on porches. They are close to it, feel it in the July heat, smell it in the corn, hear it in the clacking of the corn leaves but they do nothing, they neither welcome it nor dismiss it, they sit paralysed with their own awareness.

I was raised on lies. There are none more powerful than the lies of the mother. My mother's lies were as natural as her milk. She lied about everything. It was her nature. Fear made her lie, and cunning made her successful at it. She never hid her lies from me; I was her conscience as she was the conscience of her mother. She didn't like her daughter, Ruth. She preferred the company of men, unlike most women. She knew Ruth would grow into a woman she could not trust but she knew my loyalty was unshakable. The blind trust of the son. I was seven when I saw her come out of the Carlton cinema with the man. I was on the mitch from school. She looked happy. I didn't understand why she was coming out of the pictures with a strange man but I thought of my father at work reaching into a corner to finish a ceiling. I knew it was wrong and I knew not to say anything. I had no mother from that day on. I looked at her like she was a movie star, observing her. I watched her live an automatic life at home. I watched her work and talk. My mother talked endlessly. But she was not living in our home, she was acting a life she had constructed and it was flawless. I never hated my father for his stupidity but I couldn't feel sorry for him either. Without bitterness, I felt he was living the life he deserved. I learned the value of silence and observation. Rarely is there a need to ask questions. Words can say whatever they like but bodies can't, bodies can never lie with any conviction.

I was sure my mother would be caught, or that she would be killed in an accident but that didn't happen. She simply left. I remember hearing the famous story of the woman on the radio saying her husband went out for cigarettes one night and didn't come back. I didn't believe her, it's one of those stories that exist forever. The woman was in love with her story, in love with the rejection. My mother didn't smoke. She just left. I was sure, too, that my father would meet someone right away. Men don't like to be alone. They always meet someone. He didn't. He just kept working and Muriel helped with us. He never lied to us. She isn't coming back I don't think, he said, but I'm not sure. We'll just get on as we are. There was a programme on the telly my mother liked called *Quicksilver*. I loved watching it with her. The man

who did the programme was called Bunny Carr and my mother
said he looked like a rabbit. He didn't but she knew it made me
laugh. Give yer man a carrot will ya, she would say. Jaysus, RTE
must pick out the most stupid cunts in the country for that quiz,
they never have to give much away. Coinín Gluaisteán she called
him. I always thought she would write me a letter. *Dear Stephen,
you understand. I know you know about the world and you know about your
own mother and it doesn't matter about the rest of them.*

She wrote no letter. She thought I was as stupid as the rest of
them. Women work on the assumption that all men want is a
fuck and that listening to men and nodding at men is enough. But
I could see through women and had none of it, none of the
learned ignorance, the convenient confusions they propagate.

My father painting. I was devoted to him. The grace of him on
a ladder, reaching up to dab paint into a cornice. There was
always the right amount of paint on the brush. I would foot the
ladder for hours watching him, waiting for a drip to fall from the
hairs of the brush. Drip, I would say on the few times it happened. I didn't know the word perfection but perfection
describes his work. He measured a room for wallpaper simply by
walking into it, and when he papered it he only ever measured
once with the first length, then he would cut the rest with the
large scissors without even looking at what he was doing. It was
as if everything was in his fingertips and not his eyes. Ruth didn't
see the work he did with his brushes. He used wallpaper and
paint to cover ugliness in the way my mother used lies.

I am the last one to drive onto the ferry. There's a salty freshness
in the air; it seems hard to imagine it's still New York I'm breathing.

A loud colourful crowd playing Frisbee. Another crowd playing croquet. Everyone seems to know everyone else. Adirondacks scattered on the sloping lawn like tired swans. A redhead threatens to throw the Frisbee to me and I turn away before her gaiety forces me to join them. I sit and watch, memories of customers running through my mind. That Jewish woman who kept changing the colours just so she could devour Gerry with her eyes for an extra couple of days. A waiter asks what I'd like. A bucket of stout, if you're paying, Muriel used to say. Wineglasses stand on the arms of the abandoned chairs. Too hot for wine.

—Lemonade. No ice.

Each choice is a battle. Why New York is impossible. I regret the prospect of the lemonade. I could handle a vodka. For the sake of calmness. He comes with the drink.

—What is so difficult about remembering lemonade with *no* ice?

The waiter nods without apology.

—Tell you what: why don't you trot back and bring me a Pimm's cup.

—Ice?

His voice is friendly, his expression unreadable. I can do nothing but admire his polite rudeness.

—It always has ice.

I look away. I hate this kind of money, people on the edge of the really big money. I regret coming. A hammock is swinging between the trees. A woman's leg trailing to the ground. A silver shoe at the end of a slim leg. Fireworks go off suddenly but she doesn't move. I scoop the ice out of the lemonade and take a gulp. A young child spread-eagled on her chest. She scratches his back and he giggles. His head hides her face from view. He giggles again. The ruby ring on the finger. I swallow the rest of the lemonade. I feel caught, naked. Florent has teamed with the redhead in croquet. He laughs too much. He waves a welcome to me as if he only saw me the day before yesterday. The weekend is elaborate foreplay for him. As soon as the waiter comes with the Pimm's I take the drink wordlessly and walk away, over to her. Halfway over to her I shout back to the waiter, Hey. Good Pimm's, more as a warning to her than as an apology to him.

I stand between her and the sun, my shadow falling across them. The child lifts his head and scowls at me. She smiles, as if she knew I was coming.

—Have you noticed the grass is so green here? Shamrock green. Emerald green. Paddy green. Green as the Irish themselves green. Take a seat.

The playfulness of her tone is so disarming that I almost believe she has expected me to arrive at this very moment, as if everything has been leading to this. I sit in the adirondack beside them.

—Coleman and I were just discussing that, weren't we?

Coleman, child runt, nods his skinny head resentfully.

—There are only two homes on the island to ignore the summer drought laws. The guy who owns Victoria's Secret and our host. What does that tell you?

—People come here to feel decadent without having to actually do anything. Fallout from the AIDS generation.

—Concise and comprehensive. Who knew? Thanks for the explanation, Stevie.

—How are you?

—I'd love a cigarette.

I take my jacket off and take a cigarette out of the pocket.

—Ugh. Not Parliaments.

I put the cigarettes back in my pocket and drape the jacket over the arm of the chair.

—It was a joke, Stevie. Remember irony.

—Sister of bitterness?

She smiles and tickles Coleman. He giggles into her neck. She picks up my jacket and takes out my cigarettes. She caresses the fabric of the jacket and nods approvingly. She taps the cigarette box on the child's head and takes one out. I try again.

—So. How have you been doing?

—I've been doing. Y'know, New York. You have to keep doing. How have *you* been doing? Sorry about your sunburn.

—One layer burns off and another appears. You know the way I am.

—No. I have no idea the way you are.

Coleman tugs at her.

—Can we go for a ride in your car Auntie?

—Coleman, why don't you go and see how long you can hold your breath in the pool?

She glares at me and clings to the child. Auntie. I wonder is he related, if her family are here. I didn't even know she had a nephew.

—Go away, handsome.

—You left Gansevoort Street?

—This is true.

She looks at me, waiting for me to go. I wait. Silence was always the best question with her.

—It was time. Listening to the hockspit of prostitutes lost its charm. It just seemed to get complicated—living there. I'm gettin' old kid.

I could have had a life with her. Anyone could see that. And a decent one. She wasn't tied to Gansevoort Street after all. She just needed to be pushed. I could have done that: opened my mouth and demanded it of her.

—I think we will go for that ride, Coleman. Hey, Stevie, hold our hammock?

She winks at me.

—Chill out. Once around the park is better than nothing. Always too serious. Your stuff is boxed in Claremont if you want to pick it up. I was tempted to dump it but I couldn't do that to the books, even your books. I told the doorman there might be some Irishman coming by one of these days.

—In Claremont Avenue? You're with that dealer guy?

—Nope. I'm not *with* anyone. Claremont is mine sweetie.

She smiles as she lifts him off her and swings herself out of the hammock, smiles like a chess player savouring checkmate but it makes no sense unless it is a game, as if life is some game to her. *I grew up with screaming.* New York is lost there and then with her walking towards the house with the child's hand in hers.

I sit in the car with the door open. Ruth and me sitting in the car on Dollymount strand. I have not thought of her in a long time. Maybe I have been playing a game without fully knowing it. There is a knock on the passenger window and I jump, expecting to see my dead sister. Holfy walks around to my side of the car. A reprieve. A confession that she was joking.

—I stole your cigarettes. By accident. Good luck, Stephen. We'll be long enough dead and gone. Live well.

I say nothing and don't look at her when she walks away, don't want that to be the last image of her. I pull out the pack of cigarettes. I'll have to stop smoking. In the cigarette box is a card with a scribbled note.

We shall not cease from exploration
And the end of all our exploring
Will be to arrive where we started
And know the place for the first time

I close the door and start the engine. There is time still to make the five o'clock ferry.

The apartment on Claremont Avenue is paintings and light. Nine rooms. I wander through it as if it's a deserted film set. The boxes are in one of the back guest rooms overlooking Grant's Tomb. I open one, then another. They are packed neatly, too neatly for her to have done it and my temper rises at the idea of some stranger filing my tastes away, fingering my life, evaluating it, drawing a picture of the personality that made these decisions. I am leaving New York, have left it already. The film is over, the theatre empty. Everyone has gone, getting on with their lives. Catholicism. No, not that, too easy to blame it all on that. There is no one watching. God's bitter joke. Acting a life as if there is someone who cares as much as you do yourself. I phone three thrift shops but none of them will come collect. I take the elevator down and ask the doorman if he has any use for some books and clothes. He eyes me, looking for the catch. Explain it's either that or the trash can, none of it's going to Ireland.

Getting off the train at Crewe I walk over to the timetable to see what time the connection to Cardiff is and laugh out loud when I realise Crewe is not in Wales. I had promised my father I'd never set foot on English soil. He'll forgive the accident. I have to speak to her, to lay eyes upon her. Too long have I run from it.

I imagine what every abandoned child must imagine, I imagine the conversation. The confrontation, the reconciliation, the settling of the score, the rejection, the emptiness when nothing comes of it.

On the connecting train I stare out the window to see signs of England fading and at last glimpse a motorway sign in both English and Welsh, a reminder that like Ireland, England has conquered but lost, that tribes outlive their oppressors.

Cardiff is full of rugby fans, drunk and singing. I get a room in a small B&B only when the owner is certain I'm not a rugby fan. Mr. Parker tells me I'm far too late for supper but recommends a local pub. I walk down the street and find the bright depressing place and have a pint and a sandwich. I go home and sleep well with the tiredness of the journey in me. In the morning I get up and go and buy a map of Cardiff. I could ask Mr. Parker but his friendliness decides me against it. Too many questions. I have the address, it's only a matter of finding it. I decide against a taxi, wanting instead to walk, to feel the streets she has walked for over thirty years without us. I expect to meet her every time I turn a corner. The house is on a decent street and my heart lifts that she hasn't fallen back into the poverty that she climbed out of with my father; then disgust. She has done well, lives comfortably, happy all these years without us. It's a terraced house, small garden full of flowers. I hope she answers the door so I won't have to deal with him, hope he answers the door so I'll get to see what was so much more attractive than her family. I will ask for her by her first name if he answers, be as casual as possible.

I push in the iron gate, close it behind me, stand on their welcome mat, stare at the door, breathe deeply, look around to see if anyone is watching but the street is empty. They're all either at the rugby or watching it on television. Maybe he is at it, a big-bellied Welshman cheering his team. I lift the door knocker and rap gently and then see the doorbell. I stand back, waiting. Footsteps on a hard floor. The door opens and a man looks at me smiling. He is plain but gentle looking. Unimpressive. About sixty. Full head of grey hair.

—Is Lily in?

I expect a question, a rebuff, but he smiles and turns calling her name in a strong Welsh accent. She comes out and suddenly it's happening too quickly. I expect her to be wiping her hands on her apron, the smell of cooking behind her. She's wearing jeans and a jumper, hair still red, and she is smoking and this startles me more than anything. I never remember her smoking and the cigarette, more than the years on her face and in her movements, alienates me. She smiles, frowns, smiles again, then recognises me. She looks back at him walking down the hall into what must be the kitchen. She walks towards me, puts her hand on the edge of the hall door and tells me to come in, the accent tinted with Welsh. She closes the door and we are standing close to each other, close enough for me to breathe her in. She walks ahead of me into the sitting room. Thickened with age.

—I'll be back in a minute. I'll just get him to put the kettle on.

She leaves, closes the door behind her. I look around the room, glad I dislike their taste in gold-lined wallpaper, heavy oak furniture, and floral carpeting. Cream embroidered doilies on the arms of the sofa. They deserve ugly taste. I imagine her telling him who I am and his worry. She comes back and sits on the sofa, facing me.

—How are you?

It's as if the minute outside has given her enough time to recall exactly how she planned to handle this if it ever happened.

—Grand. Daddy died last year. Ruth two years before that.

I didn't mean it to come out as badly as that and suddenly the obvious hits me, that we are the last two and I want to rush on and tell her that I am no orphan returned but I bite my lip. I suspect she must have heard. She looks away to the door and back at me.

—I just wanted you to know. I don't know why. Just so that you'd know. She had cancer. I just wanted to tell you so you'd know. I've no bad intentions. And I wanted to see you and ask you why you left. That's all.

—You've got an American accent.

—You've got a Welsh one.

—I left because he bored me. He was a good man. It's not a very nice reason but it's the truth. There's more than that but if you want the short answer that's it. I couldn't have handled raising the two of you on my own. I knew he'd do a better job, that he'd meet someone else.

I nod, deciding not to tell her, prefer my knowledge of him over her ignorance, prefer that to flattening her with the guilt of the truth. She didn't deserve him.

—So what about you? Did you marry? Have you children?

I shake my head, want to tell her nothing; in my desire to lie to her I realise I haven't the strength to make the effort. I feel too much disgust. A phone rings softly and is picked up. His voice is quiet as if he is talking in a morgue. I abhor this other lived life. She has had two simultaneous existences, the absent presence that lived in our home, and this one here across the water with this Welshman talking quietly on the phone. It's all so pedestrian, so banal. Tedious details that add up to nothing. I stand up as he walks in with a tray, she looks at him, says nothing and he, in return, is silent. He steps farther into the room, enough for me to pass him. I walk out into the hall, walk across their tiled hall floor, open the door and turn to them both.

—All the best, Lily.

—Goodbye son.

—Goodbye *mother*.

Walking up the street I resist the urge to turn around, and as soon as I reach the corner I turn sharply and walk quickly. I walk for about twenty minutes until I find the city centre.

The ferry back to Dublin is quiet. Standing at the back on the viewing deck I stare at the ferocious wake churning in the sea. Son. Son she said. Bit late in the day for that. I search for a cigarette, jostle the keys in my pocket. Evenings when she lit a cigarette and perhaps wondered about us. I look at the keys, remembering each one: Bath Avenue, An Tigh Bocht, Gansevoort Street, Lone Tree, my father's house. Homes everywhere and nowhere. Already hot in my palm I finger the silver fish on the key ring. Lobbing the keys grenade-high into the air I wait to see them splash on the surface, but they disappear in the widening sea furrow, too quick for the eye to catch. I imagine the metal cooling on impact and sinking slowly through defiant waves, sinking, settling on the seabed.

ACKNOWLEDGMENTS

Thanks to the late Brother McNally for his encouragement during my secondary school education; Brendan Ward for his advice in Monaghan and his support in New York; Kathleen O'Malley and Alan Bergeron for their kindness and friendship; Will Irwin for his wise counsel and unstinting generosity; Dr. Susan Lohafer, the most gifted teacher I know, whose commanding intellect is matched only by her gentle nature; and Jennifer Barth at Henry Holt for her careful editing and gracious manner. Finally to my agent, Beth Vesel, for the *maybe*—Mazel Tov.